# BURNING
## WATERCOLORS

# Praise for Ginny Schuyler Warren and *Burning Watercolors*

"As a licensed clinical social worker who works primarily with a traumatized population, I found this story to honestly reflect the deep complexities that are present in abusive relationships and systems. So often we are quick to simplify both the etiology of abuse as well as the experiences of those violated, and yet Burning Watercolors speaks to the complicated nuance of finding yourself in an unsafe situation with someone who, despite being abusive, is also someone you've hoped and longed to do life with. Warren writes about the internal conflict in a way that increases compassion for those who've had to wade through this specific pain and offers a view to the reader of what a validating community looks like. There is no direct and certain formula for healing and yet the validity of art and equine assisted therapies are profound for those working through trauma, and, as a clinician I loved seeing these modalities emphasized throughout this story." — Melodee Gentry Bosna, LCSW

"***Burning Watercolors*** is a powerful, emotional insight into domestic violence and children affected by trauma and family dysfunction, for anyone wanting to understand how women are pulled into—and trapped in—marriages defined by abuse, why children with trauma often develop challenging and disruptive anger and destructive behaviors, and what can truly heal dysfunction and bring a healthy, emotionally stable future. A must-read for anyone who works with women and children of abuse, neglect, and trauma. ***Burning Watercolors*** vividly and personally brings to life the realities for far too many women and children who are emotionally and physically battered, seeing no hope or real healing in conventional therapies. Forgiveness, vulnerability, hope in the Father, and healing through relationship can change families and the world for generations to come." — Melissa M. Tenpas, MPH, Director of Royal Family KIDS Colorado Springs, a ministry to abused and neglected foster children

"***Burning Watercolors*** by Ginny Schuyler Warren is a deeply personal novel that reveals the impact of spousal abuse on both a mother and a 5-year-old son in the family. This author did a masterful job of writing the thoughts and feelings of the mother and the son. I especially liked the Point of View of the boy. The language and thoughts fit a 5 year old completely. This might sound like a gloomy book, and parts of it are hard to read, but it's actually a story of redemption. Ginny brought not only the relationships alive, she created wonderful settings as well. I highly recommend this novel." — Lena Nelson Dooley - multi-published, award-winning, and ECPA, CBA, and *Publisher's Weekly* bestseller

"Excellent group read for educators. With tender delivery, Warren illustrates reasons behind students' disruptive behavior and solutions to help restore them to wholeness." — Michelle Strom, NBCT (National Board Certified Teacher – Language Arts)

"Trauma is rarely advertised, but its effects are evident in the behavior of victims. With simple honesty and true to life character voices ***Burning Watercolors*** hits hard on fears of abuse and pull of hope. It is a powerful reminder to "Be kind, for everyone you meet is fighting a hard battle." - Philo" — Megan M. Hawbaker, RN Flight for Life Colorado, Royal Family KIDS Camp Nurse

# BURNING WATERCOLORS

Ginny Schuyler Warren

**GOTHAM BOOKS**

**Gotham Books**

30 N Gould St.
Ste. 20820, Sheridan, WY 82801
https://gothambooksinc.com/

Phone: 1 (307) 464-7800

© 2023 *Ginny Schuyler Warren*. All rights reserved.

No part of this book may be reproduced, stored in a retrieval system, or transmitted by any means without the written permission of the author.

Published by Gotham Books (April 28, 2023)

ISBN: 979-8-88775-220-4 (P)
ISBN: 979-8-88775-221-1 (E)
ISBN: 979-8-88775-222-8 (H)

Because of the dynamic nature of the Internet, any web addresses or links contained in this book may have changed since publication and may no longer be valid.

The views expressed in this work are solely those of the author and do not necessarily reflect the views of the publisher, and the publisher hereby disclaims any responsibility for them.

# CONTENTS

## PART I

Chapter 1
September 27, 1988
1

Chapter 2
March 1965
5

Chapter 3
1986
8

Chapter 4
Summer 1966
11

Chapter 5
1968–1975
13

Chapter 6
1970–1974
18

Chapter 7
1977–1982
24

Chapter 8
Summer 1983
27

# PART II

Chapter 9
August 25 – 27, 1986
33

Chapter 10
August 1987
38

Chapter 11
August 20, 1987
42

Chapter 12
August 1987
45

Chapter 13
November 1987
50

Chapter 14
March 1988
55

Chapter 15
July–September 1988
59

Chapter 16
September 27, 1988
66

Chapter 17
September 30, 1988
72

Chapter 18
September 30, 1988
76

Chapter 19
November 1988
79

Chapter 20
December 2 – 7, 1988
85

Chapter 21
December 8 –10, 1988
88

Chapter 22
December 24, 1988
93

Chapter 23
December 31, 1988
96

Chapter 24
January 7, 1989
99

Chapter 25
January 1989
103

Chapter 26
February 1989
107

Chapter 27
April 1989
111

Chapter 28
April 1989
113

Chapter 29
May 3, 1989
116

Chapter 30
May 4, 1989
119

Chapter 31
June 1989
122

Chapter 32
June 1989
126

Chapter 33
June 1989
133

# PART III

Chapter 34
June – July 1, 1989
139

Chapter 35
July 2, 1989
147

Chapter 36
July 2, 1989
151

Chapter 37
July 2, 1989
157

Chapter 38
July 3, 1989
165

Chapter 39
July 4, 1989
168

Chapter 40
July 11, 1989
172

Chapter 41
July 12, 1989
175

# PART I

# CHAPTER 1

## September 27, 1988

> Children have never been very good at listening to
> their elders, but they have never failed to imitate them.
> —James Baldwin, *Nobody Knows My Name*

"Here are my clues. It starts with P. It has faces. It was on the floor. The police taked some," I tell to my class. "Andrew." I point to him to guess.

"Is it GI Joes?" Andrew says.

"Nope," I say. "That doesn't start with letter P." I point again. "Maddie."

"Polly Pocket?" Maddie says.

"No!" We all laugh at that, but that does start with P—twice.

The class is stumped. "Ethan, show us what's in your bag," they all say.

I pull them out of my brown paper bag. "Pictures of me and Momma!"

Mrs. Perkins says, "Does pictures start with P? Yes. Good one, Ethan! Okay, that's the last show-and-tell for today, so, boys and girls, quietly go to your desks."

We go, and that's when I hear Dad in the hallway. My throat

bones get tight, and I stare at the door. I grab my scissors and throw them. "Go away!" I throw more things at the door. "Go! Danger! Danger!"

Mrs. Perkins grabs my arm.

I yank away and run to the if-bad-guys-come hiding place. I smash into a kid's desk by accident, and all the stuff inside it falls onto the floor.

Like a turtle, I hide under Mrs. Perkins's desk and put my hands over my head. My whole self shakes. I think of hide-and-seek cabinet at my home. Mrs. Perkins takes my hands off of my head. "Ethan, why are you afraid?"

"My dad! I heared him in the hallway!"

Mrs. Perkins says, "Ethan, there is no danger here at school. Your dad can't come here."

The principal comes to get me to the office. I sit on the love seat there, but I don't know why they call it that 'cause you sit there when you are in trouble. I've been in trouble before.

The principal, Mrs. Diaz, says Momma called today to talk to her. "I know what happened last night, Ethan. I want you to know that the police are watching out for you and your momma. You are safe here at school."

"I heared him, footsteps like my dad in the hallway. I heared a man voice!"

"Ethan, there are men here. You know them: Mr. Joseph, our custodian, and a teacher, Mr. Lang."

"I know Mr. Joseph, but I heared—not him!"

"Ethan, does your momma know that you brought the photos to school?"

"No, but she let me keep them in my room."

"Would you like to look at them together?"

She haves my brown paper bag and takes them out. We look at one of me at school, and I point to my dad showing in the glass door. "There he is with his camera, Jace Evans."

Mrs. Diaz puts on her glasses and looks hard at it, so to know what he looks like. She gives them back to me and says, "Stay here." Then Momma comes in.

A window in the principal's office door offers a view of the outer office where Ethan sits, waiting. My voice trembles as I say, "So, in addition to what happened today, has Ethan had conflicts with his classmates?"

"Mrs. Evans, let's sit," Mrs. Diaz says.

"You can call me Kate." I take a seat.

Ethan's kindergarten teacher, Mrs. Perkins, looks down at her chalk-covered hands. Neatly set chalk-colored hair obscures her face. "Ethan is involved in every conflict in his class."

"Is he hanging around with kids who are setting a bad example?"

"I'm sorry, Mrs. Evans. He's the instigator." She sits up straight, and her brown eyes lock on mine. The floodgates open as she speaks. She says things incongruous to her singsong, kindergarten-teacher voice. "The other students don't want to sit next to him. He talks constantly and makes distracting noises. He throws his pencils, scissors, his chair. His morning kindergarten class is several days behind our afternoon class because of the extra time I spend reining him in. Ethan doesn't miss a beat, academically or otherwise. When he's talking during my instruction time, he can repeat to me what I have said verbatim. He's smart as a whip, but he interrupts the other students' learning with his behavior. This morning, he thought he heard his dad in the hallway, and his fight-or-flight instincts took over. It's dangerous for our other students. We have done all that we can. Maybe your pediatrician would be a good resource for you …"

As Mrs. Diaz and Mrs. Perkins discuss Ethan's infractions in more detail, only the hum of the desk fan reaches my ears. It mercifully blows their voices away, down the hall, out the double doors, into the sky.

He is not provoked at school. He simply cannot contain his fury or his fear. This little boy has seen and heard too much to remain unscathed.

I was trying to do the right thing, staying with Jace. "You need to work through the hard times in your marriage." That's what they said, the older women who encouraged me to stay with him. I finally came to the unpopular conclusion that some people don't want to be helped and it's not my job to change them. I believed those women for long enough to mess up Ethan, and now he is a problem at school.

"Kate, thank you so much for coming in," Mrs. Diaz says. Into the office, to have a meeting about Ethan—again.

"Um, I guess I'll take him home."

I grasp his small hand. He tries to wrangle himself free of my grip, but experience has taught me to hang on as if his life depends on it. It does. Free of my grip, he has run into traffic, jumped from heights, and bolted through crowds without regard for the people or obstacles in his reckless path. This child has more anger than any child should carry. He collects it all up inside him. As if he has an expandable suitcase zipper, he stuffs in more and more until he is likely to burst. And he did, today, in his kindergarten classroom.

# CHAPTER

*March 1965*

---

Death is not the greatest loss in life. The greatest loss is
what dies inside us while we live.
—Norman Cousins

---

Jace's dad worked for the railroad in Colorado monitoring coal trains—forty of them a day. He had no time for kids, no time to teach them to throw a ball or fish the river. Providing store-bought food for the table and a modest roof over their heads was his primary focus.

His wife was left to tend the children, which was most common in those days. By the 1950s, women expected their babies to live. Molly was born in 1956, and after three stillborn children, Jace came along in 1960. In their Catholic neighborhood, most families had eight to ten children, or more. God saw fit to bless the Evans family with only these two.

Molly doted on Jace from day one, and Jace thought Molly hung the moon. Despite their age gap, they were best of friends.

Snowmelt was particularly heavy the year that Jace was five years old and Molly turned nine. Bundled up against the cold one day, they sat on the bank of the South Platte River in a stiff spring breeze, tossed bunches of dry grass into the current, and watched them rush away.

"Maybe they'll land in Nebraska and plant themselves by the river there," Molly said.

Jace enthusiastically threw in a variety of dry vegetation and imagined a new Nebraska field. Then, feeling sorry for Nebraska, he threw rocks to make the Rocky Mountains grow there too.

A sudden gust picked Molly's hat right off and tossed it into the rushing river. They chased it twenty yards, laughing and yelling, "Stop, hat! Stop!" And it did. Stuck to twigs at the end of a branch, it waited for them to catch up with it.

Jace got a long stick to hook the hat, but his attempts failed.

"Daddy won't be pleased if he has to buy me a new hat," Molly said. A sturdy log held the branch out of reach. Without another word, she stepped onto it and made her way out over the torrent. She closed in on the hat, crouched, reached, and pulled.

"It's stuck!" she said.

"Come back, Molly!" Jace said.

Molly straddled the log. Shoes, socks, and pants got drenched.

"Molly, I'll give you my hat! Come back!"

The twig snapped, and Molly triumphantly stood up, sopping-wet hat in hand.

"Aha! Got it!"

Jace relaxed on the riverbank. "Come back, Molly."

That's when she slipped. The river swept her away like a bunch of dry grass. Jace ran after her for a half a mile. "Come back, Molly!"

Her body was found four miles downriver.

That's how they came to live in Palm Desert, where, Jace's mom said, "Every body of water has a fence around it." Her wrought-iron boundaries kept Jace safe from physically drowning, but his struggle to stay afloat emotionally gnawed from within. She didn't actually blame Jace in so many words, but because she was always so sad after losing Molly, he felt as if she would have been happier had he drowned instead. His dad bore his grief at a painful distance from Jace, but close to the mouth of a whiskey bottle. Jace felt as if he lost his whole family and a good bit of himself that day on the South Platte River. That was the birthplace of his rage.

# CHAPTER 3

1986

---

I cannot think of any need in childhood as strong as
the need for a father's protection.
—Sigmund Freud

---

For the entirety of Ethan's short life, I have tried to protect him from seeing the abuse. I smile and fix pancakes as Jace gets ready for work. I calmly plan out the day with Ethan; we'll take a trip to the zoo, play a game, go for a swim, or paint with watercolors.

His watercolor paints are dark from end to end. He mixes them that way to achieve the effect on paper that he has in his mind. He paints a dark cloud in the place where most kids paint the sun, and a medium-sized momma with a straight line for a mouth. A big Ethan of watery, deep-colored swirls like a tornado arrives on the paper to save the day. His paintings tell of thumps he hears in the night, fights he has seen but has no words to explain.

"What are you painting, Ethan?" I inquire.

"This is my angry," he says, fully focused on his work.

Trying to shush Jace when he's mad does nothing to protect my little boy. Who am I kidding? The bruises show, the same colors as those in Ethan's paint box. I have to get out. Jace has threatened, on several occasions, to take Ethan and leave the country if I divorce him. I'm not sure why he wants me to stay. He has an image to uphold, I suppose, when it is beneficial for business. Married with a child and a house. Check.

I went to a marriage counselor who told me to keep a set of keys hidden in the car, maybe a wallet too. I took his advice. That way, I could take Ethan and leave in a hurry if necessary. Based on that advice, I thought this was, to some extent, normal. "All couples fight," they say, and "God hates divorce."

Once, when Jace was in a drunken rage, I grabbed the opportunity, when he was in the bathroom, to get Ethan from his crib and make a run for the carport. Just as I opened the door, Jace grabbed my hair and threw me to the ground, Ethan wrapped tightly in my arms, my keys still hidden in the car. The escape plan failed. Easier said than done.

We visited a counseling center for people dealing with domestic violence, once. I think it was arranged to keep Jace out of jail, but I'll never know for sure. The counselor heard our stories separately, so I don't know what Jace told them.

"Okay then. Be safe. Bu-bye," they said.

*What? That's it?* No one at the counseling center mentioned a battered women's shelter.

So, I stick it out at home and try to keep Ethan from knowing, but he's too old and smart now to not see the truth. He has nightmares. He slips into bed with me when Jace is not there.

"Momma, what if the bad guys come?" Ethan says.

"Bad guys won't come, sweetie. But if they did, I would tell them they have to leave or go to jail. Those are their two choices. And they would leave." He nods, and I hold him, but his fear remains.

I believe Jace when he says it will never happen again, but it always happens again. And Ethan paints and jumps on his bed. He "pew-pews" the "bad guys" with his finger-gun from the saddle of his Wonder Horse, bouncing the springs to their fullest potential, stretching them so far that Wonder Horse's front legs hit the floor. Thud, thud, thud.

Ethan has "imagilary" friends who stay with us "because the bad guys pewed their house. Pew-pew!"

When his daddy is gone, he climbs into my lap. "I love you, Momma."

"I love you, Ethan." He snuggles and twirls my long hair with his fingers, weaves it in and out and clutches it like a security blanket.

On Thursday through Saturday nights, I lie awake for hours, alone in bed, until sleep finally overtakes me. I often awaken at three in the morning and feel the empty place next to me. Sometimes I get up and check the driveway to see if Jace has passed out in the car. If he has, and it is summer, I'll try to help him to the house so that he won't die in the scorching desert heat when the sun comes up. I can't lift him, so if he is too inebriated to shuffle his feet to the house, I leave him half in, half out of the car. At least he has fresh air.

During those nights when I can't sleep, I think, *Maybe he won't come home tonight. Maybe he will die in a drunken stupor or crash.* But when it comes down to reality, I'll save him every time. Ever the optimist, I think life will improve.

# CHAPTER 4

*Summer 1966*

---

There is always one moment in childhood when the
door opens and lets the future in.
—Graham Green, *The Power and the Glory*

---

The summer of 1966 was a turning point in my childhood. I allowed it when I grasped the metal handrails. White-knuckled, I climbed the rungs of the ladder and counted them, ten. I shuffled along the board to the end of the handrails, then knelt to crawl to the end. The full forty pounds of me pressed my knees into gritty sandpaper texture and shredded my skin. I trembled from head to foot as I stood, rubbed my palms on my swimsuit, and peered down to the drain.

I have long forgotten the name of the boy who called from beneath me, "Once you jump, you'll see it's okay, Kate!"

He did not disclose the whole truth about this experience. I stepped off.

The air rushed past. I hit the water as if it was a solid wall. It stung my outstretched arms, blasted up my nose, and engulfed me. I sank like a stone. My ears popped. I held my breath, paddled toward the light, and broke the surface with a gasp just as a teen wearing red swim trunks grabbed my arm and cross-chest carried me to the side.

"What were you thinking, young man?" said a bronze-skinned teenager with white on her nose and a whistle on her lanyard. She towered over the cowering boy who convinced me that to jump from a great height into a wall of water is a good idea.

I sputtered and blew chlorine water from my nose. Diluted blood ran from my knees to the ground, meandered through my little leg hairs, like rivers converging and flowing out to the sea. I wondered if there would ever be a time when I didn't have at least one skinned knee.

Some people love that adrenaline rush and some don't, at all. I am of the latter type, cautious by nature. Had I challenged myself to make the jump, you might think me brave. But that was not how it happened. At six years of age, I let a boy talk me into doing something I didn't want to do, and the pattern was set.

# CHAPTER

## 1968-1975

> Nobody sees a flower—really—it is so small it takes time—we haven't time—and to see takes time. Like to have a friend takes time.
> —Georgia O'Keeffe

I have no hometown. As a military kid, I was always the new girl—in a new state, new school, new house—during my formative years. Having a personality highly invested in relationships makes moves like this especially jarring. It wasn't so bad when I was little, but it was progressively harder as I grew older. Every move, I lost all of my friends and had to start over.

There is a story about a spider that spun a stunningly beautiful web that stretched from the barn door to the head jamb. The morning dew on the web caught the light of the rising sun, and it caught the eye of the farmer's wife because of its intricate symmetry. She was saddened to ruin the spider's hard work, but she had to enter the barn to milk the cow, so she opened the door and the web was destroyed.

The next morning, she arrived to find a splendid web, again affixed from door to jamb, and sadly had to break it apart to enter the barn. Day after day, the spider spun its web, and day after day, the farmer's wife tore it down. Over time, the spider got sloppy in his work. He spun a sticky but asymmetrical web. Its pattern progressively worsened until it looked like the cobwebs you buy to decorate for Halloween. He was defeated.

If spiders have feelings, then he must have felt like I did, repeatedly losing my web of friends, creating a new web in each new state. I tried different ways to fit in at each new school, once I became aware that fitting in is a thing. I assessed the culture, compared and contrasted it to what I just left, and did my best to line up.

Our moves zigzagged from coast to coast, landing at each point for a year or two: Massachusetts, Oregon, Connecticut, Northern California, Virginia, South Carolina, Arizona, Southern California. When I was young, speaking in each new local dialect came naturally. During the era when children were allowed to run free in the neighborhood, Mom always knew who I had been playing with by the way I talked.

However, local terminology tripped me up and blew my cover. I never knew whether to say chest of drawers, dresser, or bureau. Or pop, soda, or Coke. I used the term pocketbook instead of purse in Arizona, and you would have thought I just arrived from a different planet.

I thought I had my various dialects neatly compartmentalized, but in college, a linguist told me he couldn't figure out where I was from because of my mixed accents. I dropped my Ts, used the term *y'all*, and called potato bugs "roly-polies."

When someone asks, "Where are you from?" I say, "All over." I only feel as if I have a home when I travel outside of the country, like to Canada. Then I can say, "I'm from the States." There, in Canada, I feel a sense of belonging here, in the US, until I cross the border and US border guards question why I am coming in.

I guess I was ultrasensitive about this whole fitting in thing. It impacted the path I took and the mess that my life became.

With the weight of fitting in squarely draped on my shoulders, the usual woes of childhood may have affected me more than most kids. Possessing the confidence displayed by those who 'grew up here' was elusive to me. I was always on the outside of the ring of 'friends since kindergarten.'

In first grade, I was the new girl, having moved at the end of my kindergarten year. Every day at recess, a group of second-grade girls chased me into a corner of the building so that I couldn't play, and they made fun of my shoes. The mean girls captured another girl too, but after a couple of days, they let her go, "Because she is cute."

My dad taught me how to fight them off because that's how you handled playground bullies in 1966. We practiced at home, and I was ready the next day when the time came to defend myself. That day, when they grabbed me from behind, I elbowed them in the ribs and stomped on their feet with my hideous shoes. It only took one recess to deter them. After that whoopin', they stopped bothering me, but it was a shallow victory because I was still the not-cute girl at my new West Coast school.

Two years later, living on the East Coast, I was on a girls' camping trip. A group of boys camping near by asked us to play capture the flag. The team captains were boys. We all stood in a wide row while the boys sized us up and selected us by pointing a finger.

As I am a believer in letting the chips fall where they may and letting children learn to solve their differences without too much adult intervention, you might think I am okay with this method of choosing teams. I am not. I much prefer that someone in a position of authority divide the kids in an A-B pattern. Maybe he balances the teams according to the children's ability, but the better athletes, or spellers, or whatever are not picked first, and the kids never know that selection wasn't random.

We stood shoulder to shoulder and then spaced apart as the number of us remaining dwindled. The adults who stood near me pointed out, "How interesting! That team is picking the cute girls, and the other team is picking the girls with long legs so that they will win." Interesting indeed. I was picked for the team with long legs. "We better win." I walked toward my team to play a game that was completely unfamiliar to me.

The private girls' school I attended in third and fourth grade was tough academically, but the girls were kind and inclusive. School uniforms made fashion a nonissue. French class was required, which I thought was *vraiment genial* (really great.)

During the sticky, Virginia summer, I'd savor an ice cube wrapped in a paper towel as a snack. I alternately sucked on it like a Popsicle and rubbed it on my forehead, letting cool drips run down my face. We picked plums from our tree. Their sweet juice ran down our arms, mingled with dirt from playing outside for hours.

During the winter my sister Erica and our neighbor Deanna, shoveled snow to the edges of the patio and flooded it to make a skating rink. We selected figure skates from a large collection kept in laundry baskets in Deanna's basement. We practiced our routines for days, and then we charged a nickel admission for our families to come and watch our Ice Capades. Deanna's big brother said Erica and I were good, but Deanna was like Peggy Fleming. We'd giggle, and I thought it was sweet how he elevated his little sister like that.

Skeletons of trees sprouted the tiniest buds on the tips of their fingers. We took our ice skates to the ponds, laced them up tight, jumped from the bank over melted edges to solid ice, and chased the fish we could see beneath. Frozen streams connected the ponds, and we glided along them, jumping off tiny waterfalls to the next pond down.

The weather warmed up, and when the cicadas chirped, the moving boxes arrived. We picked delicate cicada shells from tree trunks and marveled at their intricacy. Thousands of them covered sidewalks and trees, so we didn't mind when my little brother, Trey, accidently crunched them in his baby hands.

This home was where, for the first time, I tried not to become too attached to my friends. I was old enough to know we would move in two years, so I prepared for the loss by not getting in too deep. We had a lovely, carefree time. I was ten when we left.

# CHAPTER 6

## 1970-1974

> Good habits formed at youth make all the difference.
> —Aristotle

The public school in Tucson, Arizona, was a stark contrast to the private girls' school I had just left. It swarmed with loud, dusty, preadolescent males much too grown up for their own good. Their manner showed nothing similar to the Opie Taylor types I knew in second grade, when I last attended school with boys. They smoked pot and had a going-steady club with the cool girls who met at the back of the field under trees with canopied branches that touched the ground, making a room for all kinds of things done in private. Academically, I sailed through my fifth-grade year, having completed the same curriculum the year before, but I was socially naïve.

I tolerated going to school, but I really lived after hours. My sense of adventure grew, and I explored the desert, mountains, and washes. Because I am his oldest, Dad taught me to shoot and took me on hunting trips. I liked duck hunting in Northern California the best.

After two years in Arizona, we didn't move. I didn't know what to do with my relationships, so I switched friend groups and did everything I could to make my pink bedroom more grown-up. At the age of thirteen, I told my mom, "I wish I could stay thirteen forever." I gained confidence, and life was good.

In 1974 my best friends were Becky, Jen, and Paige. During school, we spent our free time running, laughing, and spinning the merry-go-round as fast as we could, learning about centrifugal force through scrapes and bruises.

We created the school's first cheer line, without a coach. We cut out letter Ts from red fabric and attached them to our white shirts. We sewed our own skirts and made pom-poms of red and white yarn for our shoes. We practiced our marching routine, humming the tune the band would play, and won first place Elementary School Marching Ensemble in the forty-ninth annual Tucson Rodeo Parade.

We square-danced in gym class, and everyone was required to pass the President's Physical Fitness test. Because we were never sedentary and daily climbed fences and swam, everyone passed the test. We thought it was a silly waste of time.

I had a horse named Arwen, meaning noble maiden. Riding my bike at lunch hour, I went to the stable to feed her.

After school, my friends and I rode to the drugstore for a milk shake. We tied our horses out back. We played a song or two on the jukebox, enjoyed our shakes at the soda counter, and then headed for the desert or our elementary school field. Our classmate, Toby Griffin, had a dirt bike and a key to the gate. He let us in, and while he groomed the baseball diamond, dragging the wide rake behind his dirt bike, we galloped around the large grassy field. The warm sun made our horses glisten with sweat and tanned our skin.

Our laughter echoed through the outdoor hallways of the school. They were actually just sidewalks with a roof, providing us easy access to drinking fountains flowing with warm, nasty-tasting water, with stains and chewing gum in the basins, and crusty calcium deposits on the waterspouts. We drank our fill and splashed each other to cool down.

When Toby finished his maintenance job, he raced us across the length of the field. Freedom blew through our hair. I reveled in the unity I felt with these girls and these powerful beasts.

Walking back to the stables, we chatted and breathed in the earthy aroma of our beloved animals.

We had secret names for each other, bridge club names: Gladys, Thelma, Edna, and Bea. We had to speak with a southern accent when we used them. And we had French names: Colette, Brigitte, Genevieve, and Angelique. We had to speak French and act very sophisticated, which was hard to pull off in our cutoffs and halter tops, smelling of horses and sweat. Our French language ability was limited, to say the least. My favorite phrase was *"Je ne comprends pas"* (I don't understand). In character, we acted out dramatic scenes as if on stage. We thought we were so funny, but really, we were just normal.

Back at the stables, once the horses were watered, groomed, and fed, I rode my bike across the valley, then up the mountainside, where dry washes crossed a roller-coaster street, and finally to the dirt road that led to my driveway.

"Hello? I'm home!"

"Hi, Kate!" Mom called from the kitchen.

I flopped onto my bed with a smile on my face and feeling of happy exhaustion.

When we moved, that all came to an abrupt end. I once again found myself as the new girl.

## *1974–1975*

The day after eighth-grade graduation, I found myself in my new home in Palm Desert, California. The three months of summer dragged.

I painted, which helped to pass the time. My paintings

transported me to places I could not go. Aquamarine washed over the page. Then I swam through it, looking at fish in bright colors, seaweed flowing, anemone, and starfish. I swam up and cracked the bright light at the surface and blinked water out of my sunstruck eyes. When the painting was complete, I tacked it to my wall next to Peter Max's *Peace* and Georgia O'Keeffe's *Red Poppy* and *Blue Morning Glories*.

Peter Max was the coolest artist I was aware of. I tried to draw his pictures, or something like them, with colored pencils, but I found them too precise, too controlled. Bold outlines contain colors in stark contrast to those next to them.

Georgia O'Keeffe's art is realistic in a free-flowing way. Her masterful ability to combine reality with surrealism is inspirational. The colors of her flowers have boundaries, but within the boundaries, they are somehow free. I imagine that's what heaven is like, only more. Free, but an actual place. In heaven, we will be able to really see everything because we will have time.

Georgia O'Keeffe said, "I found I could say things with color and shapes that I couldn't say any other way—things I had no words for." So did I.

The paintbrushes stood in rows of bottles on my craft table. They beckoned me to explore with them. Sometimes I'd get lost for hours in my watercolor fantasy. As darkness came late this time of year, I was unaware of the passage of time.

I met some kids in the neighborhood who were my age. I heard about this guy, Jace, who was away on vacation but would be back for school in the fall. I heard that he was *so* cute and funny and great—and a good kisser. That made me really nervous because I had no experience kissing anyone but my parents, my little sister and brother, and Grammy and Pop-Pop.

These city girls were sophisticated, for real. They plucked their eyebrows, kissed boys, wore high-waisted pants, and had Great Gatsby-inspired haircuts like Mia Farrow in the movie. The last time my hair was short was in second grade, and it was a pixie. I wasn't going back to that, and hot rollers were out of my realm of expertise. Therefore, I kept my 1960s-style, long, straight hair.

In the fall, my new friends were all in a frenzy, getting new clothes for homecoming, something else I never knew existed.

"You have to dress up," one of the popular girls said.

"Okay, I'll wear my high-waisted corduroys."

She laughed so hard she nearly burst.

Note to self: Maybe that's not dressy … or cool. I just didn't know how to navigate this new California life of mine at all.

One emotional teenaged day, my mom came into my room to find me crying over a song, "At Seventeen" by Janis Ian.

I learned the truth at seventeen
That love was meant for beauty queens.
And high school girls with clear-skinned smiles
Who married young and then retired.
The valentines I never knew
The Friday night charades of youth
Were spent on one more beautiful
At seventeen I learned the truth.

The song is painfully long, and the lyrics struck a chord with me. Although my family thought I was wonderful, the world told me otherwise. I opted to believe mean girls and foolish grown-ups rather than my family who loved me. The good times during my childhood were far more plentiful than the bad, but I allowed those distressing moments to shape me.

A seed of insecurity took root in my heart, playing capture the flag at camp when I was nine years old. Six years and two moves to new states later, Janis Ian sang about my insecurity for the entire world, and in 1976, it won a Grammy Award.

Jace was around and became part of the group. He didn't even notice that I existed until sophomore year.

One time, he said, "How did I not notice you last year? Were you ugly or something?"

Yes, that was it. Why would I have even given him the time of day?

He continued, "Well, you are cute now, and a girl from your middle school told me you were popular there."

*Really? I didn't know that. I mean, I didn't know that I was popular, or in that group, or whatever.* Flustered is all I can think that I was at that moment, but then we went steady.

Didn't it seem weird at all that he checked into my past with the only other person from my middle school who had apparently moved to Palm Desert too? What are the chances of that? And why didn't I check into his past? That would have been a good idea. But nope, I just let him lead me along. My naiveté caught up with me and probably contributed to my lack of judgment at this juncture. I had him, Jace Evans, the guy all the girls told me about that first summer in Palm Desert. He made me laugh with his quick wit and impromptu physical comedy. He was smart and cute, and he thought I was pretty. That was enough to make me fall for him, as a fifteen-year-old girl. I finally felt as if I fit in.

And then he wrecked my life.

# CHAPTER 7

## 1977-1982

> The world is a dangerous place to live—not because
> of the people who are evil—but because of the people
> who don't do anything about it.
> —Albert Einstein

Jace hit me for the first time about two years into our relationship. We were still in high school. His violence escalated with each incident, but months passed between times. Then he tried to beat a confession out of me for cheating on him with a mutual friend, Barry.

I escaped on my bike and sped down a busy street to a well-lit corner of a major intersection. The wide streets offered plenty of space for someone to pull over to help me without blocking traffic.

Jace caught up with me and pulled me off of my bike. He knocked me into the grass by the sidewalk where he pounded me with his fists, completely enraged over something he imagined. People stopped for the traffic lights—cycle after cycle, secluded in their cars—and averted their eyes. No one objected while Jace took out his fury on me in the spotlight while a hundred cars passed by.

I managed to scramble away and pedaled to our friends' house.

I told Barry and Janet that Jace thought I was cheating on him with Barry.

"Dude, are you kidding me?" Barry shouted when Jace appeared in the doorway.

Jace burst inside. "Don't lie to me, man! Where were you last night?"

Janet answered, "We were home, Jace. What are you thinking?"

"I know he's always had a thing for her, and I can't trust her," Jace said.

Emboldened by present company, I said, "Can you trust Barry? Can you trust anyone? No. You can't, Jace. Why do you think that is? Maybe because you can't be trusted?"

Jace lunged at me, wild eyed, growling. He dragged me, kicking and screaming, to the bathroom where he shut us in and choked me against the door. My feet dangled above the floor.

Barry and Janet yelled, "Jace, stop! Let us in." They pounded the door with their bodies, but it was a solid, old door, and it didn't break or budge.

"Jace," Barry shouted. "Nothing ever happened between me and Kate!"

Helpless, I tried again to wiggle out of his grip. He wouldn't kill me. I didn't think so anyways.

"Why do you do this? Why do you make me so mad?" I felt a light spray on my face as he screamed at me. A feeling of fuzziness came over me. My eyes closed, and blackness enveloped me. His voice grew faint. I was far off, watching from a distance. Jace let me drop to the ground. Landing with a thump, I gasped.

Barry and Janet pushed the door open.

Life would go on.

"Dude!" Barry said, "Ya can't be doin' that! Are you okay, Kate?"

Barry and Jace went to the porch to smoke some weed and chill out.

Janet helped me wash my face and brushed the grass from my

hair. We heard Barry reprimand Jace, and Jace calmed down as he took another drag from the joint.

"Kate, you have to get away from him," Janet whispered. "You don't deserve this kind of treatment. We know it has happened before." She brought me a bag of ice for my face, and I thought of summertime, ice cube snacks, and the carefree little girl I once was.

Jace promised it would never happen again. He said that he loved me so much that it made him jealous, and it made him imagine things.

"That's not love, Jace. Nothing about it is justifiable," Janet said.

I knew she was right. I don't blame him for my poor choices, but he could talk me into just about anything. I stayed with him through high school.

We both went to Arizona State University. There, I grew up, I quit partying, and distanced myself from the lifestyle Jace lived. I was a good student and poured myself into my studies. We dated each other off and on, and he was kind to me. Before I graduated, we were expecting a baby. We got married before our son, Ethan, was born. That's the respectable thing to do, right?

# CHAPTER 8

*Summer 1983*

---

> Your abusive partner doesn't have a problem with his anger; he has a problem with your anger. One of the basic human rights he takes away from you is the right to be angry with him ... The privilege of rage is reserved for him alone.
> —Lundy Bancroft
> *Why Does He Do That? Inside the Minds of Angry and Controlling Men*

---

The monsoon season was a welcome relief from the sweltering heat in Tempe, Arizona. I was up twenty-five pounds, and a tiny human's heel kicked me in the rib, day and night.

Summer school seemed like a good idea, in order to get more credits completed before the arrival of my baby, but I wondered if I had taken on too much. I went to class in the morning, worked on homework, and then took a nap.

When Jace found me asleep with no dinner prepared, he was furious. "Hey, Lazy, what have you been doing all day?" he shouted.

"I—"

"Look at this place. It's a mess. Why don't you clean thoroughly?

Take a toothbrush to the baseboards! I'll teach you what happens to slackers!"

He slapped me hard on the side of my head, and then he turned toward the closet. I guess he reconsidered his teaching method due to my huge belly. It's scary that he had the presence of mind to stop himself and come up with a different plan of attack in the middle of a rage. It was as if a switch changed him into someone else, and this person was calculatingly mean.

"What do you like?" He scanned the room for something of value to me. He pulled several of my blouses off of their hangers.

"Stop it, Jace! Stop!"

He took my favorite and tore it to shreds. His face was red, and his veins popped out. He was wild-eyed as he turned to the closet again. I took the opportunity to run out the door. When I got down the street, I hid in a wash.

Tears trickled down my face and mingled with raindrops. I nestled myself further down the embankment for more cover, but not so far that I might not be able to hoist myself out of the gully if a flash flood came. A thicket of trees, unlike most of the desert, provided my hiding place. My oasis. I heard my name called repeatedly. His voice got closer. A stick poked my side, but I remained motionless, silent.

As the sound of my name slipped farther away, the rain subsided and the sun sparkled on wet leaves. I curled up in the sparse grass, exhausted, and closed my eyes. I stayed awake, listening.

After a couple of hours, I thought he had probably cooled down and I went home. I had nowhere else to go—no family in town, my college friends went home for the summer—and I don't know to this day if battered women's shelters even existed.

Ethan was born during a peaceful interlude when I thought things would be okay.

Jace and I shared hobbies, but he really led the way. He was a skilled potter and threw pots late into the night. I glazed them, and we accumulated a large collection over the years. They were our everyday dishes, mugs, mixing bowls, and storage containers with lids. He was able to make them thin as porcelain but with the rugged good looks of ancient relics. We'd eat dinner in the pottery shed with Ethan nearby in his Moses basket, lulled to sleep by the hum of the potter's wheel and our quiet conversation.

Those evenings, his thoughts often turned to his sister, Molly, and he'd tell me again about her drowning. "I'm glad we don't live in the cold. Whenever I travel to a place where there is a cold wind at my back, I can hear her voice and see her slip into the raging river. It plays like a video in my head. I try to rewind it and change the outcome, think of things I could have done."

"Jace, you were a child. There was nothing you could have done. You are not to blame," I'd say.

"Hm. Tell that to my mother." He ran a wire under the wet clay of the pot he was throwing, took it into his hands, kneaded it on the counter, placed it back on the wheel, and then coxed it into a new form. That's when I realized that to him, the clay was his story, reformed, reshaped in his mind, with a different outcome. He just didn't know how to transfer that into his daily life. Molly wasn't coming back, and he had no control over that reality.

Jace also brewed beer. He preferred dark lagers, and I developed a taste for various beers along the way. He crafted one for me, flavorful but lighter than his others. We often sat around the fire, out back, and enjoyed dinner and a beer with friends who told him that he should open a pub. That would have suited him, but he preferred to give the beer to friends in exchange for the home-cooked meals they brought.

I'd nurse Ethan while Jace made up my plate of food. He'd bring it to me and say, "We have the most beautiful baby in the world."

Those were the best of times, the reason I stayed with Jace, trying to recapture that peaceful essence. But that was my perspective. Looking back, I know that the undercurrent of Jace's rage was just below the surface, even then.

# PART II

# CHAPTER

## August 25 - 27, 1986

---

For every minute you are angry, you lose sixty seconds
of happiness.
—Ralph Waldo Emerson

---

"Seriously, Jace, you can't leave a loaded hand gun on the coffee table!"

"Ethan can't pull the trigger, Kate!"

"Yes, he can, and it is right within reach. What are you thinking? I can't even go to the grocery store and trust that you will take care of him!"

"You are so negative! You never support me! All you care about is Ethan." Jace's face reddened with anger. He took another swig of his beer.

"What am I supposed to support? You're drunk half of the time, you're irresponsible with Ethan, and who knows where you are all night?"

"That's just what I'm talking about. You're so critical! I feel as if I have a noose around my neck when I am with you, Kate!"

"Fine then, just go on out. I'll stay home with Ethan."

Ethan stops playing with his Tonka trucks when he hears me say his name. He shuffles over and grabs the hem of my dress.

Jace storms out the door.

"When's Daddy take me Toys 'R' Us?" Ethan says.

"Not right now, Ethan. Maybe later." I take a deep breath to keep the tears in check and go to the kitchen to make PB and Js for our lunch.

Ethan stands on the couch and rests his head on its back between his outstretched arms, money from his third birthday in hand. Every time he hears a car driving down the freshly chip-sealed street, he looks to see if Jace has come back to fulfill his promise to take him to buy his birthday present from Grandma and Grandpa Evans. By the time Jace gets home, Ethan has been asleep on the couch for two hours.

"Let's go, Ethan!" Jace says through the open window on the front porch.

Ethan pops up, light brown curls stuck to his cheek with sweat, until they blow free toward the window in the swamp cooler's breeze. He slides off of the couch and runs to the front door. I open it for him. Jace reeks of booze.

"Jace, you can't take him now. You can't even walk a straight line," I say.

"Yes, I can!"

"Okay, do it. Show me you can walk the line in the driveway." I point to the control joint in the center.

He stumbles and swerves toward his car, mockingly tiptoeing along the line.

"C'mon, little dude." He picks up Ethan to put him into the back seat. His eyes are bloodshot, and his left eyelid droops a little more than the right.

"Jace, you can't take him," I say.

"I was just driving, and I was fine!" He drools a little as he speaks.

"You were just walking and *not* fine!" I say.

"It's only like two miles to Toys 'R' Us. It'll be fine!"

"No." I grab Ethan, and Jace pulls him back.

"I wanna go Toys 'R' Us!" Ethan screams. He squirms, kicks his feet, and pounds my shoulder with his fistful of dollars.

"Look what you're doing to him, Kate. You are hurting him—just to get back at me!" Jace's words are slurred, and his hateful gaze pierces my heart.

"I am not doing this to Ethan! You can't take him until you are sober." I yank Ethan out of his arms. I must have surprised Jace because he usually has really quick reflexes. I rush into the house and lock the door while Ethan sobs and mutters something about dinosaurs and a shovel, with a tight grip on his birthday money. His face is red and wet with tears, but I don't see anger in his eyes this time, just pure heartbreak.

Ethan has Jace's eyes, mostly green. Gold starbursts encircle the pupils, and dark blue forms an outline on the edge of the iris. Their eyes are like four matching stained-glass windows, masterpieces. Behind the stained-glass window of Ethan's eyes, I see a kind soul, as if sunlight is shining through them.

Jace's eyes look as if a cruel presence took up residence in the shadows behind the stained glass. The sunlight has gone out.

Jace peels out of the driveway and skids around the corner. I don't see him for two days. His mother, Grandma Evans, comes over with a casserole and talks to me about being more supportive of my husband. I don't tell her what's really going on in our home, but I feel as if I am losing my life, minute by minute as the battle rages. Ethan's life perspective is just taking shape, and I worry it is skewed.

"Ethan, come 'ere," Momma tells. I come there.

"Grandma Evans is going to take you to Toys 'R' Us to spend your birthday dollars!" Momma tells.

"Yay!"

I get my dollars quick, and Grandma takes me in her big car called Buick. It has a funny smell of seats. I stick my head out the window and, ouch, the hot metal burns my chin. Wind whooshes up my nose. I scoop air with my hand out the window all the way to Toys "R" Us. I see Giraffe up high, so I know we are there.

Toys are far and everywhere! I fast walk with Grandma Evans. I smell her perfume what smells like honey, but not the kind what is in the squeeze-bear bottle—the real kind what Momma and Dad got me at the fair with wax comb.

I wish everyone could have a grandma, but Momma doesn't 'cause they go'ed to heaven. I have two, and two grandpas, names Grandma Evans and Grandpa Evans, and G'ma and G'pa, what have Momma for a kid.

We find dinosaur row. I get a bone kit and a shovel to dig them after I bury them. I am gonna to be a dinosaur hunter when I grow up. Three things; dinosaur hunter, Toys 'R' Us guy, and a man what stands in the street with the word sign—S-T-O-P. I am not allowed in the street 'til I grow up. I do that rule 'cause Momma tells it.

Grandma Evans tells, "Let's get something extra." I like that, so we put some extra in our cart, like Play-Doh and Hot Wheels. Grandma puts me in cart to play with Hot Wheels, and she pushes to the leaving place. I give the man my birthday dollars, and Grandma gives more dollars. Then we take all home to play.

Grandma drops off me and then leaves to a salon to get her permanent.

"What's permanent, Momma?"

"That means it lasts forever."

"Then why she have to go there all the time?"

Jace comes home two days later with a six-pack of empty beer bottles in his hand, tosses them into the trash and helps himself to leftover pizza.

"Daddy!" Ethan drops what he's doing and jumps onto Jace's lap.

"Hey, Ethan! I missed you, but I don't think mom wanted me around."

"Don't put words into my mouth, Jace!" *Here we go again. At least we had a couple of days of peace.*

"Want to help me wash the car?" Jace says to Ethan.

"Yes, yes, yes!"

I catch glimpses of them, and they are having so much fun together that it gives me a moment's hope. Ethan runs his rag around the hubcaps and giggles when Jace sprinkles him with the hose. They finish, and Jace sends Ethan inside and drives off. I am left with dinner to make, laundry to wash, and a crushing feeling that the Jace I loved is lost to me forever.

# CHAPTER 10

*August 1987*

---

*Once you learn to accept the truth, no matter how painful or heartbreaking it is, you'll stop wasting time on the wrong people.*
—Sonya Parker

---

Months pass—holidays, birthdays, ordinary days—full of turmoil. In early August, when Ethan is almost four years old, I find myself trembling all the time and have dropped so much weight in one week that a neighbor questions whether I am okay. *No, I am not. I'm a wreck.*

My hope for things to get better isn't going to change anything, so I come up with a plan to find out once and for all if I can make my marriage to Jace work.

Perched on my kitchen stool, weaving the coiled phone cord through my fingers, I wait for Gwen to answer. "Hey, Gwen, can you watch Ethan tonight?"

"Sure, girl! What's up?"

"I'm playing detective, and I don't know how late I'll be."

"Okay, but be careful, ya hear? Just bring him around whenever.

You can pick him up in the morning. I'm not doin' a thing tonight. James isn't even in town."

"Have I met James? No matter. Thanks, Gwen!"

I fix myself up, put on a sundress that I like from two years ago, and then drive Ethan over to Gwen's.

"You smell nice, Momma. I brung my Hot Wheels for me and Carson, and jammies like you said, and toothbrush. Where are you going?"

"Just out for a while. Now, you be good. Do what Miss Gwen says." I kiss him goodbye. "See you later, alligator."

"After while croc," he skids to a stop before running inside, "o-dile! Hi, Miss Gwen! Thanks for the sleepover! Love you, Momma ... Car-son!"

"Call me when you get home, Kate, so I know you're okay."

"Okay. Thanks again!" I call over my shoulder.

I stop at a few happy hour spots close to home. When I don't find Jace, I drive to a bar in Palm Springs that our friends frequent. Young men in pastel boat shoes and girls in spandex miniskirts populate the admission line. I stand in it, feeling frumpy in my sundress, inching my way to the door. *This could be a big waste of time. What will I do if I see him? What if he sees me first? Maybe I should leave.*

"Why the frown?" a preppy guy in a Polo shirt with an upturned collar asks. He has a friendly smile.

I smile back at him in spite of my misery.

The bouncer unhooks the velvet cable to allow more people inside, checking IDs.

"Kathleen ... this doesn't look like you." He obviously doesn't have the keen eye of border patrol officers who can recognize you in a nine-year-old passport photo.

"Well, I have a perm now, and I was happy when the picture was taken." I feign a cheery disposition. "See? It's me."

"Go ahead." He reaches for the ID of the preppy guy behind me.

Trying to look pleasant, I search the crowd for a familiar face.

"Kate! Hi!" It's Liz, who is not really a friend, but we have friends in common. "Jace is over there."

I make my way to him, and he grabs me around the waist, turns me around, and plants a big kiss on my lips. "Hello, Kate. What brings you here? Want to dance?" He hustles me to the dance floor. That's when I see a group of smirking girls with big, puffed-up hair behind him. We dance for one long song a few inches apart, and I have never felt so distant from him—not even alone in my bed at night.

When we leave the dance floor, the smirking girls approach.

"Hey, Jace. Every time I see you here, you're with a different girl," the apparent ringleader says, shifting her too-big shoulder pads.

"This time he's with his wife!" I say, heavy-hearted.

The realization that my suspicions are accurate punches me in the chest. It hurts too much for me to be able to savor the moment the girl's face falls into a look of confusion, then anger. I think for a moment. *What do I do with her? Who is she—an innocent victim of Jace's charm and deceit?* He's wearing his wedding ring, so she cannot be oblivious. Neither can any of the others. As I look around for an escape route, every laughing woman I see is laughing at me. Every girl in the whole place has competed with me for the attention of my husband, and won. Did Liz know? Does everyone?

"You know what, Jace? I'm done with you!" I turn on my heel and choke back tears.

Jace reaches for my hand. "They are just friends!" His eyes plead with me to believe. The girl with the shoulder pads slaps him hard and confirms that he's lying.

The preppy guy glances my way as I run away from the whole ugly scene. Locked inside my car, I sob.

*Tap, tap, tap.* I wipe my nose and eyes with a tissue and roll the window down.

"Are you okay?" It's the preppy guy. "I saw you leave, and, I mean, I saw what happened. Are you okay?"

"Yes. I will be, anyways. Thanks."

He stands and spots his friends leaving. "Sure?"

"Yes." I sniff. "I'm going home. Thank you."

My reality has taken a turn. As my world crumbles, I ponder what is real in my life. At least, from now on, I won't be living the lie, trying to drive away negative thoughts that, as it turns out, are true. Determination creeps in where devastation used to live. I drive home, envisioning a different life than the one I thought I had when I got up this morning.

Miss Gwen lives in a big house with not so much fruniture. She tells we can ride in play cars indoors when it is too hot outside, like now. We have races, and I take Carson's little sister, Monique, for a drive in a red and yellow one. We don't win the race 'cause she puts her feet down onto the floor tile when I go fast.

When we have dinner, I ask Miss Gwen, "Why did Monique and Carson's dads go away?"

She tells that's not important why they divorced. But they love their kids because that is something that can't get broked, not all the way. She tells that sometimes, big people have things inside that are broked. Maybe you can't see any love left at all, but there is always a part in their heart for their kids.

I picture my dad's heart with all different parts made of dark wood blocks. I picture the blocks all knocked over and one tiny block for me. It is light-up. I don't know how, but it is light. I wish the other blocks are light-up too, one for Momma, and one for G'ma and G'pa. Dad has much dark.

I think I have much light-up blocks in my heart.

"Miss Gwen, I have a block in my heart for you. It's light-up."

Carson is very quiet. That never usually happens.

"Carson, I have a light-up block for you too."

Grateful blocks must be light. I have grateful for my friends.

# CHAPTER 11

*August 20, 1987*

---

Jesus loves the little children
All the children of the world
Red and yellow, pink and green
Funniest kids you've ever seen!
Jesus loves the little children of the world!

---

"Sing with me, Ethan, or the tickle monster is gonna get you! Ahhh! Tickle, tickle, tickle!"

"Mom-mahahaha!"

The morning sun peeks through the bedroom curtains. The bottom half of a birthday cupcake is on my nightstand. Leftover from Ethan's fourth birthday, it made its way from the kitchen to my bedroom sometime close to when Ethan made his way from his room to my bed, last night—a curious coincidence.

"Is it true?"

"What, Ethan?"

"That Jesus loves the children?"

"Yes, Ethan. It's true."

Ethan rolls his little body across my bed and slides off the end until his feet touch the floor. "Carson's mom said dads just leave."

I think of my friend Gwen raising her two children on her own. "Um, I guess she thinks—"

Ethan interrupts, "Do you want my dad to leave?"

"Ethan, come here."

His feet don't move any closer. He hangs his four-year-old self over the foot of my bed, toes still touching the floor. His lower lip sticks out as he forms his thoughts carefully, then says, "I don't want to divorce." I wish that word never entered his vernacular.

"I know, sweetheart. It makes me sad too, but Dad is going to stay away for a while. We'll see what happens, okay?"

"Not okay! Not okay!" Ethan wipes his tears on the bedding. He hasn't noticed that Jace has already been gone for four days. "It not permanent!" he says and buries his face in the bed spread.

I had prayed for an opportunity and the strength to do whatever it would take to be free of him and his abuse. On a calm morning, free of conflict, opportunity presented itself. Jace was still in bed, and I gave Ethan his breakfast. I slipped away to the bedroom and, with the door closed, I said what I needed to say. I didn't have to jab Jace in the ribs with my elbows or stomp my shoes into his feet. I simply said that I was done living like this, told him he could stay wherever he was until five o'clock all those mornings, and ended my brief speech with a quiet but firm conclusion that changed the trajectory of my life: "I'm serious. You have to go."

He went.

I wonder what compelled me to do the things other people wanted me to do, such as jumping from the high dive. I suppose I was a people-pleaser by nature, and when people other than Mom and Dad started asking me to do things, I complied. Choosing to believe the lies that negated my value, my talent, and my beauty set me on a destructive path.

When I started high school, I just wanted to fit in. I wanted what I could not have: the acceptance of the mean girls, the praises of strangers, and for the cute boy who the girls told me about the summer before high school to cherish me. In the process, I gave up a good chunk of who I was.

Now my mess is Ethan's mess, and we both cry a little longer with the length of the bed between us.

# CHAPTER 12

*August 1987*

---

> Accept what is, let go of what was, and have faith in what will be.
> —Sonia Ricotti

---

"Oh, dear. I thought you had it all worked out between the two of you. You hid it well. I wouldn't have guessed." My mom takes the news with her usual grace.

We hang up the phone, and she comes right over to console us over breakfast. Ethan hops into the IHOP.

"Three, one children's menu," I say to the hostess.

"And crayons," Ethan says. He likes the crayons but leaves the yellow one at the hostess stand as we take a booth.

"Mom, I don't know what I'm going to do. Once I pay for the car, day care, food, and utilities, I won't have enough to pay the mortgage."

The coffee comes, and I hug the warm mug between sips, drinking in the energy to go on with my story and my life. Comfort comes in the little things, and with this excellent cup of coffee and my mom planted squarely across the table from me, I know I will make it. I just don't know how.

Ethan colors and eats a giant smiley-faced pancake with two flavors of syrup. It is not the usual sugar-free breakfast that I provide, but this is a special day with G'ma, and a little syrup for both of us might sweeten the mood.

Mom heard the why of my pending divorce on the phone, out of Ethan's earshot. Now she wants to know my next step. She is always good at helping me sort out problems. Usually she hears what I have to say, and when I finish talking and answer a couple of her perfectly timed, thought-provoking questions, my problem is solved. Or, at the very least, it doesn't loom so large. I don't think she will be able to do that this time.

Mom listens intently and processes all I say. "I have weighed my options, looked at housing, run the numbers, and nothing adds up to anything that will work for us."

She lays out a workable plan in five minutes flat. I guess that comes from making good choices her whole life. Her calm life and stability enable her to see things objectively. Mom and Dad are financially secure, and they are happy to help. I swallow my pride and accept the offer to stay with them.

"Until you get on your feet again," Mom said, reassuring me with a pat on the hand.

"Ethan, what's that you've drawn?" G'ma points at his artwork.

Ethan moves the blue crayon to his left hand so that he can point with his right. He holds black and brown tightly with blue so that no one can take them away. The upheaval he feels has made him a pack rat. I find things stashed in his room, in the hospital-corner pocket of his Ninja Turtle bed sheets. After Carson's birthday party, I found eight glow sticks hidden in there.

Every child was given one, but somehow, he ended up with eight. I don't know where he picked them up and didn't look inside his party bag when we left, but I imagine he smuggled them out that way. Hospital corners make a secure secret hiding place until laundry day. Stone-faced, he never fessed up to stealing the glow sticks, so I made an assumption based on shaky evidence and disciplined him anyway. That's really hard because of the nagging thought that maybe some of the other kids did give them to him, but I doubt it. He lost TV privileges, and we went to see Carson's mom. Gwen's current boyfriend answered the door.

"Hey, Richard. Ethan has something to return to Gwen," I said.

"She's out running errands. Quiet down, you two!" he shouted to Carson and Monique, so that he could hear the game on TV while he talked to us.

"I'm sorry I took these," Ethan said. He held out a fistful of glow sticks, which Richard tossed to a table in the entryway.

"All right. Gotta go. I'll tell Gwen you came," Richard said.

I really don't like that man, and I'm sure our encounter with him didn't make the slightest impact on Ethan to do the right thing in the future.

Ethan cried all the way home, and as we turned into our driveway, he said, "I hate you!" He had never said that before.

At the IHOP, Ethan tucks his feet under him in the vinyl booth and points a syrup-coated finger at a blue lady with blue hair and a big blue smile on his drawing. "That's you, G'ma, and that's G'pa, and Momma." (I still have a straight line for a smile. I need to work on that.) "That's me. I'm going high on swings."

Mom points to a black scribbled semicircle on the side of the page where most children draw a bright yellow sun. "Can you tell me about that, Ethan?"

"That's my dad, but not all. Just his *think* because he goed away from us."

I wrinkle my nose and smile at the way he expresses the facts of his life. "So, that's his brain?"

"Yes, in his head but with hair on. He thinks of us, don't you think?"

"I know he does."

As mean and callous as he is toward me, I know he has feelings for his son—just not enough character to do right by us. He simply can't think ahead or stop his impulsive behaviors and self-gratification.

The check comes as Ethan lifts his plate vertically to lick the remaining syrup. I am too drained to correct his manners. I turn to Mom and say, "This is on me. Thank you."

I have a lot to do to get the house ready to sell—small repairs and decluttering. I hope to get enough done to post it for sale by owner in the fall.

G'ma and Momma talk and talk. I color. The lady what brings the pancakes brings me yellow because she thinks I forgot it, but I didn't.

Then she says, "Do you want to know my favorite syrup?"

I do, and she tells me butter pecan. I try some, and it's pretty good. I have my pancake with three syrups, and Momma doesn't notice. I keep coloring even after I get some sticky on my picture.

I like dark colors but not being *in* the dark. I had some glow sticks to hold in my bed, all colors. If I swish them fast back and forth together, the yellow and red makes orange, and the blue and yellow makes green. Altogether, they look like fireworks without the sound. I like the fire of fireworks but not the boom. It makes my chest thump, and I think of dark. Then it comes, and the firework goes out. I had to give back the glow sticks, so then I only had my one, and that's not too bright.

I prayed and asked Jesus for more glow sticks, and for food for the babies with stick-out tummies and flies on their eyes. I saw them on TV. Momma tells we take care of one in Africa. That's far, so we won't meet her. I saw where on the globe.

Then one day, the lady what brings the mail brings me a embelope from Carson and Gwen, and it is glow sticks with writing: "We forgive you, Ethan, and you can have these." So I think Jesus must have sent some food to those babies too.

# CHAPTER 13

*November 1987*

---

Do what you can, with what you have, where you are.
—Theodore Roosevelt

---

Fall arrives, and although we don't brag about our fall colors in Palm Desert, a few Chinese Pistache trees in our neighborhood turn a brilliant burgundy. Mums give some color to the entry, and the bright green winter rye grass adds to the curb appeal. I stick the "For Sale by Owner" and "Open House" signs out, and I wait on the front porch with a cup of coffee.

The blazing sun has cooled since August, so people flock from colder climates to buy winter homes in the desert. Snowbirds increase our population during the winter months and create a great housing market for sellers.

A pretty brunette in a bright yellow maternity dress holds the hand of a red-haired toddler with curls cascading down her back like a lava flow. The man with her, obviously her husband, has a red crew cut and a calm demeanor.

"Why would you move? This house is so cute!" she says.

"We're, um, it's not my first choice, but life is full of surprises," I say.

Ethan peeks through the curtains with a pout on his face and runs to his bedroom. The family steps into the living room, and the woman gasps as if she has just walked into the Palace of Versailles. They love everything about the house, including the dinosaur wallpaper in Ethan's room.

"Angelique is really into dinosaurs!" the woman says.

She turns to Ethan. "You must be ready for an adventure. Is your mommy taking you someplace wonderful?"

"G'ma and G'pa's house," Ethan says.

"You get to live with them? Well, I can't imagine how wonderful that would be. You are a lucky boy!" She glances my way with an understanding expression.

We tour the house, and I point out the crayon lines in the mortar on the hearth where Ethan made a road for Hot Wheels. I could not get it off no matter how hard I scrubbed.

"No matter," the man says. "Maybe we'll just line the rest of the mortar to match. We have crayons."

His wife chuckles adoringly.

I show them the hole in the wall where Jace opened the door too hard and punched the knob right through.

"He's real handy. He can fix it," the woman says, tipping her head toward her husband.

*Such a nice family,* I think. I like them right away and the fact that their child possesses the name I used to pretend was mine, in the days of pretending to be French, put the icing on the cake.

I say, "The carpet has a hole under Ethan's bed, and some of the windows are stuck from forty years of paint. The swamp cooler is great, the roof is new, and the water pressure is fantastic. It's got a good foundation." My foundation might be shaky, but this house is solid.

"Sold," the man says. The woman hops in excitement and hugs her belly.

The girl, Angelique, plays with my dinosaurs. I don't want to give her all my toys. Momma tells we will take all my toys to G'ma and G'pa's house, and bed and all. Only not the house. That lady what has a baby in her tummy tells it's a adventure to go to G'ma and G'pa's, and I think it is. Now I know that we will take our stuff, so I am happy to go. Then I will have three grown-ups—not just one at my house.

We go to my friend Mae's house for watching *Robin Hood*, and then they help, well not Mae or her little brother, Brekken, but their mom and dad help to put all our stuff in boxes so that we can take it to G'ma and G'pa's house.

Angelique will have my room, but with her toys, not mine.

Our longtime friends, Janet and Barry, sprang into action the first week Jace was gone and brought us dinner. They invite us over for movie night and help me pack. Ethan and their daughter, Mae, are pals, just three weeks apart in age.

Janet had their boy, Brekken, when Mae and Ethan were two years old, and I admit, I was envious. Envy is an ugly thing, but they seem to have, obviously, what I want: great couple, great kids, great life, like the family that bought our home. The dysfunction in my life is clear to me now as I formulate concrete ideas about what I want in the future. I am happy to be on my way.

"Now that Jace is gone, we can hang out more, you know. Barry never liked the way he treated you and just didn't want to be around him," Janet says.

This is the third such comment I've heard recently. No one said a word when we were still together. People just don't want to butt into your business, but when abuse is your business, I wish they would.

"Thanks, Janet."

She smiles, wraps another glass, finishes the box, and tapes it up.

"Ethan, will you write a K for kitchen on this box?" I say.

He delightedly obliges with a black Marks-A-Lot.

Janet smiles and comments, "Kate, I just love the way you involve Ethan in things. I feel as if I'm not teaching Mae enough because I'm always so busy with Brekken, and with Barry's business's social commitments, and you know, activities."

The truth of it stings. Taping boxes and using a Marks-A-Lot to write letters is an activity we can afford. She is right though. I use what I have to carve out a productive life for us, and we don't generally feel as if we are missing out on activities. In the three months since Jace left, we have a new rhythm, structure, and best of all, a peaceful home.

The transition to Mom and Dad's house is easy for Ethan. It's familiar, and it is great for Ethan to have the three of us loving on him. He still has a rough time with Jace. Maybe he always will.

I live at G'ma and G'pa's house, and they have a pool what I like. They have a color TV what works all the time. G'ma lets me sit at the counter when she makes dinner, and I tell her 'bout Ninja Turtles. She tells those names are artists: Michelangelo, Raphael, Leonardo, and Donatello. *Hmm, artists? I don't know.*

One day, Momma tells me, "Get dressed."

Dad is coming to get me, and we are going to the zoo! I love the zoo. It has giraffes what you can pet and camels what you can ride. The rain forest is sprinkly, and we cool off in there and look at bears with glasses like G'pa's, but not, 'cause they are just lines on their face fur. "Right, Momma?"

"Right, Ethan, spectacled bears."

The petting zoo part is smellyish, but the furs are soft on those animals. One time, I laid down on a sheep. Momma telled I got poop on me from the ground, but we washed it off in the splash park.

I am ready to go, and Momma gives me my snack. G'ma comes

in from the garden and looks at the clock, then at Momma. She wants me to help her pull some weeds while I wait. I am so excited! The zoo is my favorite place, and my Dad is taking me!

Momma comes out. "Want to swim?"

Why would I want to swim when I am going with my Dad to the zoo? But she has a sad face, and I don't want to make her sad. "Awright, but when is Dad coming?"

She is not sad at me. She is sad at Dad. I know that now 'cause he is not coming. He never comes. I throw my snack in the driveway, and I scream loud—then I cry. Momma has to go to work, and G'ma goes swimming with me, but it's not the same as the zoo.

# CHAPTER 14

## March 1988

> Memories are the key not to the past, but to the future.
> —Corrie Ten Boom

Dr. Melanie Quist, child psychologist, has a large office with a window overlooking a lush garden and courtyard. She has shelves of toys, manipulatives, squeeze toys, and things to hit and pound and build. She is calm, soft-spoken, and patient.

Ethan squirms in his chair, looking uncomfortable.

"The tag, Momma." I borrow scissors and cut the tag from the neck of his T-shirt.

"Tell me about your home, Ethan," Dr. Quist says.

"It's okay." He answers, looking at his hands.

"Do you have your own room?"

"Uh-huh."

"What's your favorite thing to do in your room?"

"Hot Wheels and paint."

"I have some of those. Do you want to play with my Hot Wheels?"

"I guess so."

Ethan picks out a few cars and builds a track while Dr. Quist continues to converse with him.

"Aaaaaah! Stop talkin' to me!" He kicks the track he just put together, throws himself onto a beanbag chair, pounds his fists, and kicks his feet.

"Okay, Ethan. I'll just go over here, but I won't leave, and neither will Momma." She crosses the room and positions herself to be able to watch him as we talk. "I'm glad you and Ethan came today, Kate. From what you told me on the phone and what I see here, I would say we have some work to do. But don't lose heart. I have seen kids who have suffered trauma of all kinds become productive adults. The fact that he has always been loved will go a long way in his recovery. I see that comfort is important to him. Let him wear comfortable clothes even if that means he wears sweatpants to school every day. He will struggle to focus if his waistband bothers him or a tag tickles his neck."

Ethan has decided to play with dinosaurs and is battling with them on the rug across the room.

"I'm not going to push him today, but next time or the time after, we will discuss what he remembers of the abuse. Routine will be important to him. Don't coddle him—but do give him time to respond to instruction. He will need extra time to process any change of events. For example, give a five-minute warning when you will be leaving a friend's house or changing activities. This is a good way for any child to emotionally prepare for change, but it is even more important for a child like Ethan. He will feel as if he has more control if you set a timer and he comes to you when it goes off than if you abruptly announce, 'It's time to go now.' We can start with that."

"I thought he was so young that he wouldn't know what was going on."

I strain to hear Dr. Quist's voice. She doesn't want Ethan to hear what she says. "Kate, the hard fact is that, even in the womb, babies are affected by trauma, and by the mother's stress. We need to help Ethan deal with his fears. Even if the immediate threat is gone, the reality in his mind is that danger could occur at any moment. His emotions are on a hair trigger."

"He was more aware than I thought." I realize that I am stating the obvious. "He told me once that he thought his heart was going to break his bones."

"It almost did, Momma." Ethan looks up from his toys and then walks over to us. "It really almost broke my bones right here." He touches his hands to his throat and chest. "That's why I cried. My breath was stop, and my think was dark."

I didn't leave Jace soon enough, and I have no excuse for my stupidity. As if wrung from my heart, my tears overflow.

Dr. Quist says, "Ethan, tell me about this dark."

"I don't know. My think was just dark, and I looked—but I don't remember."

"Ethan, did you see your Dad?"

"He hitted Momma. I saw through bars."

"What bars?"

"On my bed. I have a big-boy bed now."

"You must have been very little."

"I don't remember how big. Can I play now?"

"Yes, Ethan. Can you tell me if this ever happened again? The dark?"

"Yes, lots."

Dr. Quist asks a lot of questions to me. Momma cries much. I play cars and fight dinosaurs. Roar!

Why she asks me about my baby crib, I don't know. Babies have them—and I did—but now I have a big-boy bed. I hold my bones, and I don't like to tell to her.

I look out the window and remember that my think was dark and my breath was stop. My Dad yelled and Momma cried there too. I see through bars. I remember it for a minute or second, and then I want to stop. I tell to me, but not with my mouth, just my think: *Stop*.

Dr. Quist is ask me to remember more, but I just tell, "Dark happens lots. I want to go play."

"Okay," she says.

Pain is in my think. I fight dinosaurs to death! Roar!

# CHAPTER 15

## July–September 1988

> Freedom lies in being bold.
> —Robert Frost

We live with my parents for eight glorious months. Seriously. Glorious. We've felt safe, although Mom and I both rehearsed dialing 911 and recited our address about a million times with Ethan.

I am now employed at a boutique called Tattered Treasures, which sells antiques and women's boutique clothing and has a consignment department as well. I have purchased all of Ethan's school clothes there for a small fraction of the cost I would pay at the mall, some with the original tags still on them.

In July, on the hottest day on record, we move to a patio home that is close to Mom and Dad and school. It has a patio, as the name implies, but it also has a small patch of grass and some bushes in the back yard. A large sturdy eucalyptus tree stands in one corner. The yard is not fenced and opens to a wash with natural desert and Shadow Mountain beyond that. It is at the end of a cul-de-sac and is small but really quite nice. We are making a life for ourselves, and I feel great about it.

I fix a little cabinet in the kitchen where Ethan likes to play. In it, he keeps a couple of books, a lunchbox full of Hot Wheels and Ninja Turtles, a clip-on book light, a little camping pillow, and his baby blanket, which has been washed so many times that all the color is gone. He calls it "my blanket what is white." He loves to go inside and look at books. Hide-and-seek is a favorite game, and nine times out of ten, that's where he hides.

I can cook an entire dinner while calling, "Ethan? Where are you?" I hear him giggle in the cabinet, but I draw the game out a little longer.

He's five now, and I think he is a little old to still fall for this game. However, Dr. Quist says it is normal for children who, due to trauma, have missed a developmental stage to revert to lower-age-appropriate games to fill in the gaps. One boy she counseled ran around the yard wearing a Superman cape when he was twelve years old.

She told his mom, "Let him. He needs to relive that phase in his now-safe environment."

So, as much as Ethan wants to, we play hide-and-seek and he hides in his usual spot.

After dinner one evening, we walk to 'Playground Park.' The swing squeaks back and forth, back and forth.

"Higher, Momma!"

I push him a little higher. "Push your feet forward, Ethan, now back, now forward, good! Lean back, sit up, lean back. You are doing it!"

"I am! By myself!"

I feel a chill in my bones as the September sun falls low on the horizon, although it is still ninety-two degrees. My stomach tightens as if to warn me of something I do not see.

"Let's go home, Ethan."

"Okay. Can we have a story?"

"Sure. Pajamas first, then you pick."

Once inside, I lock the doors. Ethan puts on a pajama top

frontward and his Ninja Turtle underwear backward so he can see the picture of the heroic, reptilian foursome. He picks *King Bidgood's in the Bathtub*, and we settle ourselves in our favorite reading spot on Comfy Couch. The full moon rises as I begin.

"Help! Help!" cried the page when the sun came up. "King Bidgood's in the bathtub, and he won't get out! Oh, who knows what to do?"

"I do!" cried the knight when the sun came up.

"Get out! It's time to battle!"

"Come in!" cried the king, with a boom, boom, boom.

"Today we battle in the tub!"

We read through King Bidgood's time to lunch, time to fish, and masquerade ball with King Bidgood in the tub for the duration, until finally:

"When the moon shone bright, "Oh, who knows what to do? Who knows what to do?"

Ethan is groggy now and rests his head on my lap. "I know!" Ethan says.

"I do!" said the page when the moon shone bright, and then he pulled the plug. Glub, glub, glub."

Ethan smiles, turns his sweet, moonlit face toward me, and says, "The end."

"Yep, problem solved."

I take Ethan to bed, tuck him in, and kiss him good night. "Sweet dreams."

He snuggles in and reaches for his glow sticks.

After I dry off from my shower, put on a bathrobe, and wrap my hair in a towel, I hear feet shuffling in the hallway. "Go back to bed, Ethan."

When he doesn't reply, I go to the hallway to confront him. Jace stands in the center of the hall and snaps a Polaroid picture of me. He pulls out the square photo, fans it, and drops it to the floor.

"What are you doing here?"

"I came to see my son," he says smugly.

"He's asleep, and it's late. How did you get in?"

"You have no right to keep him from me," he says as he photographs my angry response.

"What are you doing? Quit taking pictures. Are you out of your mind?"

He laughs and follows me down the hall.

"Get out!" I run to the bedroom phone.

He barges in ahead of me and yanks it out of the jack. His experienced hands grab my throat. He throws me to the floor and chokes me so that I can't scream.

Terror grips me. As I throw punches, he pins my arms down with his knees. I kick and writhe on the floor, unable to scream. Just as I feel the fuzziness take hold, he releases my throat and punches my face.

"Just admit you were having an affair with Barry, and I'll stop."

"That's crazy! I never …"

He chokes me again, and I consider fabricating a story to make him stop, but I figure it will make matters worse in both the immediate and long-term future. His grip presses my neck into the floor, and I can't speak.

Ethan stands in my bedroom doorway, his eyes big as saucers. He screams, runs toward us, and kicks Jace with his bare foot. I see him run to the kitchen, grab the phone, and dive into the hide-and-seek cabinet.

Jace's momentary distraction gives me a split second to squeeze out from under him. I reach under the bed and grab my baseball bat. I swing hard but awkwardly, and miss my five-foot-eleven-inch target. He lunges at me, and on the backswing, the bat connects with his shin. When he bends down in pain, I swing again and knock him to the floor.

He grabs my ankle and drops me. My head hits the bed frame, and I feel warm blood flowing around my ear and dripping to my neck. He claws his way up my body in the same way that a person who falls through a frozen lake scrambles along a ladder shoved out to him, as if I am there to rescue him as he is tugged into some unseen abyss. His hands cover my mouth and nose.

"Why do you make me so mad, Kate?"

This is pure crazy. I fear that, this time, this is actually going to be the end of me. I cannot reason with him. I am completely overpowered by his physical strength. If he were actually drowning, I would use the escape techniques I learned in lifeguard training. I give it a try, burst his grip with my forearms, and push with my legs at the same time. His hands slip to my waist. I knee him hard between the legs and roll out from under him as he catches his breath.

I scramble to the kitchen, call for Ethan, and grab his hand as he opens the cabinet door. We run out the front door, across the cul-de-sac, and along the sidewalk until we reach a busy, brightly lit street. We stand under a streetlamp, Ethan in his half-backwards sleep attire and me in nothing but a short bathrobe. My hair is a wet, tangled mess, my face is swelling, and both of us are panting. I scoop my boy up into my arms and squeeze him hard. I kiss his face and thank him for being my real hero.

Jace rounds the corner at the intersection on foot, spots us, and heads our way.

An elderly couple stops their car, and the man says, "Is everything okay?"

Another car stops, and another. People get out of their cars, curious to know why this wreck of a woman and her scantily clad boy are out on the streets in this condition.

Jace casually slips into the night. When the police arrive, he is nowhere to be found.

I am in my bed, playing fireworks of glow sticks under the covers. Momma buys them for me now because she knows I don't like being in dark. My glow sticks are broked in spots, but they still light. Momma's in the shower. I hear a loud crash and jingle like a broken plate. That's not funny, so I make myself flat in my bed with the covers all on, and I don't make a sound. I don't like the dark, but sometimes it has to be, Momma tells. I put my glow sticks back in my sheet pocket by the wall, and it would be really dark but the moon is a circle tonight, so I can see a little.

I hear steps and breath. I peek a tiny bit out and see someone, so I hide back. Hours and hours happen, or minutes. I hear Momma is turning off the shower. In a little while, she tells, "Go back to bed, Ethan," but I am already, so I just stay still.

I feel frozen in place, and I think my legs won't work. I hear talking, yelling, running, loud thumps. I don't like those, you know.

Now I know something is really bad. My legs do work, so I get up and go down the hall. I see … I see my dad, and I see he is on Momma, all angry and hitting. I don't think. I run and kick him like a Ninja and run fast to get the kitchen phone and whip the cord to get it down. I take it into hide-and-seek cabinet with the curly cord stretched out almost straight. I dial the number 911. Momma and G'ma practiced and practiced with me before—in case we had a fire or a burglar.

"I am Ethan Evans. My … address … is …. I forget, I forget! My dad is here, and he is hurting my momma! I think he will kill her!"

I hear Momma call my name, and I peek out with one eye. I think we are screaming, but I don't know if that is real or just inside me. She opens the cabinet and grabs my hand, and we run and run for an hour or two, or something.

When we get to the lighted-up street, a grandpa and grandma what are strangers talk to Momma. She squeezes me so I think they might be trying to take me away, but she tells, "No. They stopped to help." Then I hear her whisper, "Thank you, God. Thank you."

The red and blue lights spin and spin. Police talk to Momma, and I just watch. I see their badges and guns, and I am not scared. One says, "Are you okay, buddy?" He tells it to me, and I am not Buddy, but I am okay.

One police what is a lady asks me some questions about what

happened. I say all about it. They give us a ride home in the police car! Their radio says, "We picked up male suspect." I remember the words, but I don't know what it means.

We open the door, and I see squares of pictures on the floor. I pick up a picture of me on swings at Playground Park and one of me walking with Momma. I find one from at my school too, and Momma picks up lots more from the floor. Then she stops to wipe her eyes.

"Can I keep these?" I say.

She nods, and I tuck them in my bed pocket with my glow sticks and lie on my bed to see the moon.

# CHAPTER 16

## September 27, 1988

> Friendship is not something you learn in school, but
> if you haven't learned the meaning of friendship, you
> really haven't learned anything.
> —Muhammad Ali

The next morning, Ethan drags his feet across the school parking lot. He watches the round, orange-vested woman raise her stop sign against traffic, but he doesn't move into the crosswalk until I nudge him. His friend Dylan and another boy cozy up next to us as we walk into school. "Hey, Ethan, what did the pencil say to the pencil sharpener?" Dylan says and waits just a moment. "Stop going in circles and get to the point!"

The big boys laugh, and Ethan smiles at them as they proceed down the hall to first grade.

I walk him to his classroom door. "See you later, alligator," I say.

Ethan looks over his shoulder at me and says, "After a while, crocodile."

We pinkie hug, and I tap his head and say, "Think." It's something we have been doing for a long time as a reminder to not react on every impulse. It doesn't always work. However, after the fact, when he hasn't thought before he acts, he sometimes remembers and says, "I didn't think." I hope someday he will train himself to think first.

I leave him as his teacher, Mrs. Perkins, reminds them that it is time to join her on the learning rug.

I arrive at work ten minutes later. I love my job. Well, it's more that I love the woman I work for. Gabriella Leoni is a lot like my mom in that stable, commonsensical way. As I walk in, she does a double take at the swelling and bruises on my face. She shakes her head and says, "That man. Never feel guilty for leaving him. He left you long before he moved out of your house. Someday your son will understand."

"I still try to think of ways I could have made things work out."

"That would take two of you," Mrs. Leoni says.

I phone the school principal to inform her of the events the night before. Then I get to work, tagging a large pile of clothes for consignment. It's a good thing that Mrs. Leoni allows me a flexible schedule. When the school calls two hours later, she shoos me out the door. That's when I find myself in the principal's office—the day that Ethan's internal zipper broke and his anger burst out.

We leave the principal's office with Ethan's hand tightly enclosed in mine and stride briskly to the car. On the way home, he is stoic. Mrs. Perkins said to give him clear rules and to keep it simple, just four or five at the most. He sits down at the kitchen table, and I get out a piece of paper and a box of colorful, fine-tip markers.

"Want to choose a color for me?"

He silently chooses black.

I write:

Rules of Our House:

1. Never say or do anything that will hurt another.
2. Obey your momma.

3. Respect all property.

"Can you think of any more, Ethan?"
"Don't lie," he says in a monotone voice.
"Good thinking!" I smile and pat him on the back and write:

4. Don't lie.

"Don't steal," he says.
"Another good one, Ethan."

5. Don't steal.

Ethan sticks the list to the door of the fridge with a dog magnet. "Because we are not getting a real dog or a cat or any other mammal or a reptile, right, Momma? Can we get a fish?"

"A fish would require some care. You have to feed them and clean the tank and freshen the water. Are you going to do all that?" I ask.

"Yes."

"I'll think about it, Ethan."

"A zebra fish because his stripes will remind me of mammals, and I want to name him Pepé Le Pew."

"Perfect." I start to clean the kitchen. "Can you tell me which rules you broke at school today?"

"Rule 1 … and rule 3."

"Yes. Good. You know the rules, so what are you going to do in the future to avoid breaking those rules?"

"Think."

"Okay. Can you make your body obey what you are thinking?"

"I try, but it is hard. When can I see my dad?"

"Sweetie, it is my job to keep you safe. Right now, Dad is not safe. He is sick. You know how when Carson had chicken pox, I kept you away from him until he was better? You were sad that you couldn't play with him, but I didn't want you to get chicken pox, so

I had to insist. This is a little like that. When your dad gets better, then you can see him. Until then, I have to keep you safe."

Even as I say it, I know the day could come when a court order could render me powerless to keep that promise. I hug him tight, and he hugs me back.

"I want to write a card, Momma. How do I spell G'ma again?" He has the black marker in his hand.

"Start with a capital G, then an apostrophe. Here I'll show you. G'ma."

"If a vowel is at the end of a syllable, it says its name," he says. "What?"

"Like *me* and *go*." Ethan pointed to my word: *G'ma*. "That would sound like Jee'may."

"How would you spell it, Ethan?"

"J-ee-m-ah."

"What about Tina? That ends with letter a."

"Hmmm. Well, Mrs. Perkins says *usually* for that rule, and you can spell a name how you want to, so I guess that's okay."

"How'd you get so smart?"

"I listen. And I remember everything." He smiles, and then the expression in his eyes takes on a darkness for just a moment. I wonder what he remembers.

Dylan arrives on the school bus at three forty-five as usual with his Scooby Doo lunch box in hand. Not one to risk getting hungry, he always brings his emergency supply of Twinkies, Funyons, and a thermos full of juice, "'Cause it's good for ya." He is Ethan's best friend in the neighborhood. He comes over after school for a couple of hours every day until his mom gets off work. I earn a little cash that way after I get off work.

"Hey, Dylan," Ethan says. "Why did the music teacher need a ladder? To reach the high notes!"

They laugh as they run outside to dig for dinosaur bones in the dry wash. Later, they settle in with Hot Wheels until Dylan's mom comes to retrieve him. Tracks run from the dresser to the bed and from the bed to the floor. Roads cover most of the room, and really, what more would you want in your "imagilary" world than a fast car and lots of steep hills?

"Hi, Kate. Oh, wow! What happened to your face?"

"Hey, Suzanne. Jace came for a surprise visit. It's been a bit of a nightmare, but the police did pick him up."

"Was it last night?"

"Yes. He's been charged with breaking and entering, battery, and neglecting to pay child support. He's waiting in jail for a hearing. I will have to testify in court. They questioned Ethan. They did a good job with that. If we have enough evidence, Jace could go away for a while, but that's a big *if* because I was such an idiot I usually hid what was going on." I put a hand on the butterfly Band-Aid behind my ear. "I guess it's not too late to start collecting evidence. The police took pictures of my cut." I lift my hair to show her, and she gasps. "They photographed the broken window and groups of the Polaroids and kept some that have his fingerprints on them. Those will show he's been stalking us too."

"What are you talking about? Photos?"

"Yep. He's been following us around and taking photos, even of Ethan at school. He took pictures of me when he broke in. He left them scattered on my floor."

"Wow, Kate! I had no idea it was that bad!"

"Exactly. That's the problem." I breathe to clear my mind and will my eyes to stay dry. "They're creating a Hot Wheels world." I nod toward Ethan's room.

"D, it's time to go to soccer," Suzanne calls down the hall. "Grab your stuff."

"You get it for me," Dylan demands as he emerges from Ethan's room.

"Dylan James Turner, you get your shoes and lunchbox and go directly to the car."

He drops his belongings on the floor at his mother's feet, turns on his heel, and runs to the car. He pulls a bag of candy out of the glove box and pops a blue gobstopper into his mouth with a chubby hand. Then he offers some to Ethan, who gladly fills his pocket with a variety of sweets.

"What will you do if he comes here again … when he gets out?" Suzanne says as she absentmindedly picks up Dylan's shoes and lunch box.

"We'll see, I guess. I'm in the process of obtaining a restraining order, but really, that doesn't do much if I don't see him nearby in time to call the police. But, to answer your question, I don't know … you have to go. Coach Mike will be mad if you are late again, and that's not good, especially since you're married to him." I feign a smile.

"Kate, anything you need, anything at all, please call. Mike and I are happy to help. No more secrets! I mean it." Suzanne gives me a big hug.

They depart, and Dylan wags his blue-stained tongue at Ethan who laughs, turns to me, and says, "Rule 2."

I see Dylan at school and he tells me a joke. He is bigger than me but not as brave, probably 'cause he doesn't have to protect his mom. He is my good friend and one of the only kids at school what likes me, well, what knows me, anyways. I like that he comes over after school. We have snacks and play. I tell him that my dad came at night and did bad, bad stuff. I wonder if Dad is a bad guy for real.

I show Dylan the pictures what were on the floor when we came home after. Momma threw some in the trash and I finded another one what had me and Momma. I put it with my others. Momma telled, "You stay out of the trash!" and I did after. I still keeped the picture though.

# CHAPTER 17

## September 30, 1988

---

> Real valor consists not in being insensible to danger
> but in being prompt to confront and disarm it.
> —Sir Walter Scott

---

"Hi, Kate." My father approaches me in the garden where I am trimming bushes with an electric hedge trimmer. I find gardening therapeutic and have noticed over the years that my level of frustration is illustrated clearly in the amount of trimming the bushes receive. Today the clippings on the ground outsize the bushes left standing.

"Hey, Dad. What brings you by?"

"How would you like to go out to Indio Hills and shoot a few rounds? Mom can watch Ethan after school."

"Sure. It's been a long time." I left the clippings for later and locked the trimmer in the storage shed.

Indio Hills Shooting Facility is just thirty minutes' drive from home. We head out to the desert. The sun is hot, and a dusty breeze blows steadily, drying our sweat before it has a chance to moisten our skin.

Dad hands me my twelve-gauge shotgun. He had the stock

shortened and padded for me when I was young. I feel the smooth wood and the familiar texture of the grip. He grabs his firearm along with ammunition. I stuff my vest pockets with shells, and we head out to the sporting clays area.

Each station has a different animal or bird simulated. Clay discs are released at varying speeds and distances and fly across or away from us. The rabbit station has a target that rolls at ground level along a metal rail.

The quail station is hardest for me, and I only get one. In the past, when Dad and I went hunting, I always struggled with quail. They'd rush out and away from us as we approached their hiding places in the bushes. No matter how prepared I was, I'd jump, startled, and miss the shot.

The rest are pretty easy. I lead each target and hit almost every one.

"You're still a sharpshooter, Katie," Dad says when we round the curve to the back of the field.

"Just like riding a bike." I beam at his compliment. I know I need more practice to increase my accuracy.

I love being out with him—just as I did when I was growing up. I was always so proud that he was my father. When he left the military, he finished his medical training and became a surgeon. He took me on rounds with him to see his patients in the hospital. Sometimes I would go out on emergencies with him. I handed him instruments and gauze while he stitched people up.

One of those times, we saw several car accident victims at the hospital on the same night. The first patient was a man who was thrown through a tempered-glass windshield in a newer-model car. He had a hundred little cuts all over his face and neck that were tedious to stitch but not life-threatening.

The next patient was a young boy who was thrown into the windshield of an older-model car that didn't have tempered glass. It sliced him deeply all the way across the forehead. Dad had me apply pressure to the boy's gash with a huge stack of gauze pads, at least four inches thick. The blood soaked through and warmed my hand. I thought I was going to pass out, so I signaled to Dad that I had to leave the room. The boy's face was draped so that only the gash was exposed. He couldn't see me leave or the blanched color of my face. A nurse stepped into my place, applying pressure. I thought I was going to be sick. I went into the hallway, sat with my head between my knees, took some deep breaths, and then returned to finish the procedure. It was on-the-job training that few teenagers have the privilege to experience.

I absorbed more knowledge on those rounds and emergencies than I did in anatomy class. I am definitely a hands-on learner. Maybe that is why I had to experience life as I did, make my own mistakes and learn from them, rather than listen to and obey my parents. Or maybe I was just straight-up rebellious.

Doctors and nurses at the hospital frequently asked if I wanted to be a nurse. Later Dad would say to me, "Don't be a nurse. Be a doctor if you want to go into medicine. It's a much better job." But I wanted to be an astronaut.

Dad waited years for me to return to him, his girl, gone astray. I took the hard path in life, disregarded his wisdom, and he let me. He presented plenty of opportunities for me to turn my life around, but he couldn't force me to adhere to his teaching. Finally, he let me go my own way. However, the moment I decided that enough was enough and explained the mess I was in, he opened his door, opened his home, and opened his heart to me without a bit of condemnation.

"Katie." He falters a moment looking for the right words. "I want you to have your gun in your house. I'll give you the ammunition you need and a handgun as well. I'll buy you a gun safe to keep them out of Ethan's reach. You need to protect yourself and Ethan."

"Thank you, Dad. You're right," I say. Now that I am older and wiser, he seems to be the most brilliant man on the planet.

We pick up our spent shells as we go so that Dad can reload them at home. The wind has died down, and the faint scent of gunpowder gives me a sense of nostalgia, but more. It is the scent of safety. I stuff the empty shells into my pockets, and we walk to the next station.

Shooting through the last few stations on the course bears a weight of utmost importance. This is no longer recreational shooting. It is training.

# CHAPTER 18

## September 30, 1988

Play is the work of childhood.
—Jean Piaget

G'ma has a big yard. I help her pick up pecans that fall from really big trees. In winter, I use the long picker with G'ma to get oranges and grapefruits from high up. When I was little, I called them "blapefluits," so sometimes we are silly and call them that still.

G'ma picks me up at school. I have lunch at her house. It is warm outside so we go for a swim in her pool. G'ma has a skirt bathing suit. She calls mine britches. I lie on the cool deck to warm up, which seems like a oxymoron (G'ma tells me that word.) My skin gets bumpy, and I look like I am made of deck. G'ma laughs at that. I show her my muscles. "I am Deck-Man." I play that Deck-Man is a superhero and run all around the yard.

When I stop at the sunflowers, I see a cute, little caterpillar. He's brown and black. I let him crawl on my hands, and I call him Pilar. Pilar is my pet, and G'ma lets me put him in a jar.

Hmm, Pilar in a jar. That rhymes.

She helps me make holes in the lid with G'pa's real hammer and a nail. I put in grass and a stick for his climbing exercise and drops of water to drink. I put in leaves from the pecan tree and some bushes. I watch and watch him, but he won't eat them. I worry he might die. This is not like *The Very Hungry Caterpillar* at all.

I want to be a good dad to him, so I look for another leaf. I put a sunflower leaf in Pilar's jar, and he takes a bite and gobbles and gobbles until he is full.

"He looks excited," I tell, I mean *say*. (Momma says, "Say *say*, not tell.")

G'ma laughs at that, but I don't know why it's funny. Now I know what he likes to eat so I make a bag of sunflower leaves to take home with us when Momma comes to pick me up.

G'ma says I am a good dad. My dad is in jail.

Momma comes, and when we get home, I tell her, "Pilar wants a bigger house."

In the storage shed, Momma finds a little aquarium with a crack in the glass and puts a screen over the top. I set up a yard for him and a mayonnaise lid with water in it for a lake. He lives in there on my bookshelf for the rest of October, and when November comes, he turns into a chrysalis. I worry that he will die because of no food and no water, but Momma says it is what they do. Maybe he will be a beautiful butterfly when he comes out.

But then his chrysalis gets smaller, and we think he is drying up. It looks like a seed and it is tiny. When it is almost Thanksgiving, Momma says maybe we should put the aquarium back in the storage shed. I say, "No." I don't mean to cry, but I do. He is my pet, and I want to wait more.

In two days, he comes out! He wiggles and pushes, and I can see his wings! He flies around the aquarium with his beautiful black and brown wings, and he has white spots all in a row. I give him a new name, Pattern, because he has a pattern.

Now he is new again, and Momma says we should probably let

him fly out because he won't be happy in there like he was when he was just a little caterpillar.

We take him out at G'ma's house because I think he might remember, and he flies away into the sky. I know he is happy because he is free.

# CHAPTER 14

*November 1988*

---

Let the wild rumpus start.
—Maurice Sendak, *Where the Wild Things Are*

---

For Thanksgiving week, my extended family gathers at the cabin outside of Prescott, Arizona, for as close to a week as anyone can spare. Everyone arrives with enough food for a month.

Erica's four children adore Ethan. He tells stories from picture books to the little ones, Caitlyn and Jack, who are three years old. The big boys, Trevor who is six and Alex who is eight, wrestle with him to "grow his muscles."

They run through the forest with sticks to scare off bears and accumulate dirt, even inside of their clothes. When bath time ends, the tub and floor are caked with enough dirt to grow a garden. Toothpaste from five toothbrushes in two delicious flavors—bubblegum and blueberry-blast—is splattered and smeared in places that make me wonder if teeth were brushed at all. This is vacation, so the kids' bathroom just gets crustier with every passing day until it is time to go home.

The bookshelves at the cabin are heavy with great old books, some I grew up with and some that my parents and grandparents grew up reading. I select *Black Beauty* for the bedtime story and tell Ethan and his cousins I will read a chapter each night. Some nights we read two or three as we are drawn into the story. Black Beauty's life begins happily in his pasture with his mother, but as time goes on, life gets harder and he is mistreated. I never saw the story from the perspective I have today, but now I can relate to all of his struggles, wanting to do the right thing, but not always having things turn out how he would like because of the cruelty of others. The analogy falls short though because Black Beauty didn't have a choice in the matter—and I did.

On Thanksgiving, the men deep-fry a turkey out back and drink their dark lagers. The girls enjoy a bottle of wine and cook inside, near the fire, between turns playing Scrabble. None of us is enamored with cooking, so someone is customarily assigned the duty to pick up pies at Rock Springs, adding forty-five minutes to the drive from Palm Desert but totally worth it. Between the four of us—Mom, Erica, Trey's girlfriend, Tika, and me—we prepare the rest of the feast from scratch, and it is amazing.

Janet, Barry, and their children join us for dinner. They have a place across town, not far from our cabin, that they bought as an investment after attending Arizona State University. When they arrive, Barry stops short of the door to grab a beer with the guys. The volume goes way up when Brekken and Mae come into the house. After a moment of loud rejoicing, we send the kids outside to gather pinecones to make into turkey decorations.

The kids attach tail feathers to their pinecones, and a snood cut from construction paper with lots of drippy Elmer's glue. Each turkey gets a pair of googly eyes. We have a "Thankful" tablecloth that Erica brought, and we all write or draw on it to show our gratitude as the men bring the golden brown turkey inside. Then Mom prepares the gravy. I am thankful for my loving family and my sweet boy whose arrival is the best thing that ever happened to me. I write it on the tablecloth with an orange marker.

The kids stay up late to finish playing Rail Baron, and Ethan wins—with just a little help from Uncle Trey. The prize is a turkey drumstick, and he is delighted.

We say good night to Janet, Barry, and the kids as they get into the car. Wind whistles through the ponderosa pines, and thick clouds cover the moon. Dad and Erica's husband, Paul, bring in cushions from the deck chairs as we tuck kids into bunk beds and sleeping bags on the floor.

Once they're in bed and story time is over, the adults sit by the fire and enjoy quiet conversation as the kids drift off to sleep.

After a couple of days of sunny autumn weather, winter arrives in a glorious blanket of white. The wind has stopped, and large flakes fall like feathers, piling up on trees until their weight bends the branches and they drop their load.

We have our coffee and eat a light breakfast. Then Mom, Erica, and I bundle up and go out for a walk in the forest. Snowflakes contrast against the dark background of my sleeve, and I pause to take in their delicate beauty. Some bump into each other, creating an elongated delicate pattern, gently weaved together. Others collide, breaking off bits of the other, tangled together, the broken pieces keeping them stuck, but incongruous, as if a cat played with the threads of the weaving.

Once broken, they cannot be repaired. The delicate pieces are gone forever. The only hope is that they will melt away entirely and come next winter, re-formed in the clouds, they will drift again through the sky, made new again.

I suppose that's how it is with Ethan and me. The broken pieces are irreparable. It's going to take some tearing down and rebuilding to be whole again.

"You're awfully quiet, Kate," Mom says.

"I need to be more purposeful in helping Ethan, and I suppose, in working on my own healing too. Dr. Quist has been very helpful to us, but one hour a week is not enough. Mrs. Perkins has tried her best with Ethan, but she has twenty-six other kindergarteners to manage."

"Do you have anything in mind?" Mom says.

"No. I don't know what is available. Deep inside of Ethan is a pain I cannot reach. No amount of normal life will outweigh what he's been through. It's like he has to be rewired, and I don't know if that is even possible."

"I'm so sorry, Kate," Erica says. "I haven't been available for you. I feel bad..."

"Erica, you were having babies and living your life. I would not even want to bring you into my mess. Anyways, you can't erase what Ethan has seen and heard. He needs to let his anger out. I read an article in *Life* magazine about brain development that talks about children in Romanian orphanages. These kids can't attach because of the neglect they experienced as babies when their brains were developing those connections. It wasn't very hopeful, and it said that a piece of the child is lost forever."

The snow crunches beneath our boots. We pause to take in the beauty around us. A foggy veil formed by our breath hangs in the air; the vapor clears and forms anew with each breath, like my thoughts, cloudy, then clear, cloudy, clear.

"Ethan wasn't neglected, but he did have repeated trauma that I think affected him a lot."

We trudge through the snow again.

"Do you think it's that serious?" Erica says.

Cloudy ... she doesn't know, really, how it has been for us, for Ethan. Clear ...

I say, "Have you seen his artwork? It's terrifying. It's all dark colors. Even the paintings with somewhat happy content have a dark cloud at the top or a shady character on the edge. It's always present. He needs to get control over that darkness. Otherwise, I fear for his future.

"He's such a dichotomy. He wants to be a kind *dad* to his

caterpillar, and he's perceptive and compassionate beyond his years toward me, and toward children in poverty. Then he loses all control over his emotions and his body at school when he has to sit still or at home when things aren't going his way. He can't sit in the classroom for the hour and a half before recess, so he's disruptive to the other kids. He won't talk to me about the night Jace broke in with the camera or about Jace, period."

"Sorry. I guess I didn't realize," Erica says.

"I know, Erica. I feel as if I have the ideal setup with Ethan going Mom's after school and playtime with Dylan, who in spite of his flaws, has been kind to Ethan and respectful to me. He's really very sweet. And Ethan recognizes Dylan's disobedience to his mother, so it's kind of an iron-sharpening-iron relationship. Dylan views life from his light, sunny perspective, and I've heard Ethan tell him to be respectful to his mom.

It's a great schedule for a normal kid with a normal past, but Ethan's life has not been normal. I can't pretend that nothing has happened. I'm going to look for a program that will do more for Ethan. Dr. Quist might know of something. She must. And maybe it's time to let him have a pet. I'll start small."

Shouts ring through the trees as children with sticks approach. They make themselves big, wave their sticks in the air, and stomp their terrible feet to scare us away. We growl and show our terrible teeth and hold up our terrible mittened claws and say, "You are wild things! Roar! Growl!"

They giggle and run toward us, little feet stumbling through the snow. They throw themselves onto the fluffy, white ground in pretend exhaustion, flap their arms and legs, and "cheep-cheep" their little voices, creating a flock of snow angels.

The beasts have been tamed by our show of strength, and we all go back to the cabin for turkey soup.

Packing up to go home is always a noisy production. The children are still playing and running through the house, sort of helping, but not a lot. Piles of dirty clothes are shoved into garbage bags. Everyone takes a task: vacuum, wash dishes, pack coolers with food. Bedding is changed, and bathrooms are cleaned. The three big boys bring in cushions from the deck and stack them inside one last time. The little ones pick up toys and books in the play loft.

As I make the final sweep of the bedrooms, I look under beds and in closets and pick up stray socks and Ninja Turtles. I spot *Black Beauty*, tuck it under my arm, and we head home.

# CHAPTER 20

*December 2 - 7, 1988*

---

I have not failed. I've just found ten thousand ways
that won't work.
—Thomas A. Edison

---

I'm exasperated. Ethan is anxious, angry, and fearful. He alternates between lashing out and brooding.

Mrs. Perkins calls after school one day to say, "I don't know if you are planning on using Ethan's school pictures as Christmas gifts, but they will not be good. He was angry and would not smile."

When he comes inside from playing, I say, "Can you explain to me what happened at school pictures today, Ethan?"

"They combed my hair, and I didn't want it combed. The comb was in a glass of stinky watery stuff. Blagh!" Ethan makes a face like he had just sucked a lime.

"So, do you think G'ma will want to put your school picture on her fridge with Alex's and Trevor's?"

"Well ... I don't know, but I didn't want my hair combed."

When the school photos arrive, I pull them out of the envelope and burst out laughing. Once I regain my composure, I call Ethan into the kitchen.

"How do you like these pictures?" I say.

"They're okay. But my hair is dumb."

I buy the whole package and get a frame for the 5 x 7 to put on our mantel. Ethan's face has a furrowed brow, and his lips are pursed together and sticking out. He is very mad in the photo, but we both love it. Ethan chuckles at his angry expression.

Ethan is happy playing at G'ma and G'pa's and when he's with Dylan and Carson. However, at school, or when I have to enforce structure at mealtime, homework, or cleanup, he is often uncooperative and sometimes downright obnoxious. He's fearful in the dark and has frequent nightmares. He still says he's afraid of bad guys.

Dr. Quist says that children who experience repeated trauma or abuse are in a constant state of elevated fear, expecting further danger at any moment. Because of that, they react to small triggers in exaggerated ways, which are often socially unacceptable. Therefore, when all the children in line for school pictures cooperatively get their hair combed, Ethan overreacts to that trigger and is furious. They also tend to imagine, more than most children, monsters in the dark.

I search for programs to help children who are trauma survivors but find none. Dr. Quist doesn't know of anything beyond traditional counseling that has a proven track record of effectiveness. You can do more therapy sessions or have less-frequent visits. That's the extent of the options. I decide to create my own therapy. I think of two activities for Ethan and me to do together: horseback riding and watercolor painting.

In order to pay for it, I get a job as a waitress on Saturday nights. The steakhouse always needs someone to fill in on weekends because most of the girls want to go out. Mom watches Ethan, and because I get off work at midnight, she drops him off with me on Sunday morning after church. That gives me two and a half extra hours to sleep in.

In spite of research that says not to expect full recovery for children who suffer trauma in early childhood, I have hope for Ethan. I find a place that has an opening for us to ride on Saturday mornings. The man I talk to on the phone sounds laid back and smart. When I hang up the phone, I can hardly wait for the first Saturday in January.

# CHAPTER 21

## *December 8-10, 1988*

---

> Our many different cultures notwithstanding, there's something about the holidays that makes the planet communal. Even nations that do not celebrate Christmas can't help but be caught up in the collective spirit of their neighbors, as twinkling lights dot the landscape and carols fill the air. It's an inspiring time of the year.
> —Marlo Thomas

---

My life feels like a roller coaster—and not in a good way—but I'm determined to have a wonderful Christmas. Ethan's excited about it too, and I am happy to see him smile more often.

I'm at the top of the ladder, and Ethan helps me keep the strands of Christmas lights untangled as I pull them up and staple gun them to the eaves. We have big multicolored bulbs, like most people, nothing too elaborate. Our Christmas tree has multicolored lights as well. I love the warm glow they cast.

Our neighborhood is about half Jewish, so the white and blue lights on their houses for Hanukah are a cool contrast to our warm colors. I love that we all decorate at the same time of year. I recall that, as children, my friends and I shared stories of traditions and talked about Hanukah gifts my Jewish friends received each of the eight nights. It just made the buildup to Christmas all the more fantastic.

We've just started hanging the lights when Ethan drops the whole strand. Several break on the concrete walkway.

"Ethan, don't try to pick them up. I'll get the vacuum."

Once that's done, I replace the bulbs with the leftovers.

"The pattern is wrong," Ethan says.

He is right, but we don't have the colors to make the pattern. I've always made it red, orange, yellow, green, blue. Repeat. Jace liked it that way.

"Well, let's just do a crazy pattern that doesn't repeat at all. Help me unscrew some and switch them around."

If Jace comes by, he will freak out. Good. We create a chaotic pattern with zero repeats. We even commit the heinous crime of putting two of the same color side by side in some places. When the strands of discombobulated lights are ready, we attach them to the eaves. Then we hang a pine wreath on the door made of boughs we cut off the bottom of our Christmas tree. Mr. Snowman, our plastic friend who's the same height as Ethan, stands next to the front door with a light bulb in his back to make him glow.

The sun has set, and we step back to look at the festive sight. Some bulbs point up, some down, and some stick straight out. It looks, well ... like a six-year-old did it.

"I hope G'ma and G'pa come see it tonight! They will love it!"

"They will love it, for sure."

They actually are coming over because Dad has an aquarium he said we could have.

Ethan is in his pajamas when they arrive.

"Who did the lights?" G'pa says.

"We did! Aren't they awesome?" Ethan says.

"They are the best I've seen!" G'pa says.

G'ma takes Ethan to read his bedtime story in the living room, and Dad and I set up the aquarium in Ethan's room on the shelf where Pilar the caterpillar used to reside. Ethan's story is finished, and he helps pour the blue gravel he chose into the aquarium. We'll run the filter a couple of days before we add fish. The light glows softly, and the hum of the motor makes white noise that I always found soothing when I had my aquarium as a child.

Two days later, Ethan and I pick up Carson and Dylan and head to the pet shop. The puppies in the window are the cutest ever, and we stop to watch them.

"Christmas is when most puppies are bought, and about three months later, many are abandoned. Kinda like bunnies at Easter," the pet store employee says as he picks up a fuzzy one and scratches behind his ears.

They are so cute, but we can't afford one from that store. The employee hands each boy a puppy. They wiggle and lick and pee on the floor. They jump on the boys' legs and wag their cute little tails. I wish I could get one.

Ethan has the same thought. "I wish I had a dog, just a little one what could sleep in my room."

"Someday, Ethan."

The boys put the puppies back in their box, and we move on to the fish. They each select a few: angelfish, zebra fish, neons, and orange goldfish. Then they pick out a treasure chest, a sunken ship, and fake seaweed.

When we get home, I tell the boys that we need to float the bags of fish in the aquarium. "We have to be sure to give them time to acclimate."

When everything is set up and the bags are floating, the boys go out to the gully to play.

I lie on the couch and gaze at the Christmas tree. My eyes wander from one ornament to the next; I savor each memory they conjure up.

My fish are so cool. I did name one zebra fish Pepé Le Pew. I love my aquarium. I still wish for a dog, but that's okay. Me, Carson, and Dylan are playing wild horses, and we go out to the desert past the gully and a little ways up the trail on Shadow Mountain.

"I'm rearing up to stomp a snake!" Carson stomps the imagilary snake.

"Let's gallop to the top of the mountain," I say.

"Yeah!" We run up the trail our fastest. We get to a place we call Resting Rock and sit. We can see the city from here. It is getting dark. Christmas and Hanukah lights are on almost every house. I see my house and my tree in the window.

"I hear rustling in the bushes!" Carson says.

"Maybe it's a bear!" I say.

"Maybe a tiger!" Dylan says.

A furry creature pokes his head out of the bush.

"Ha-ha. It's a jackrabbit!" Carson jumps up to see it, and we all go too.

Rabbits always run away, but this one stays. I walk over and see it is not a rabbit. It is a little dog, with hair what is white, but dirty so it looks gray. I look at the parking lot where another trail starts, and it has no cars parked.

"Come 'ere." We all call her. Dylan has a snack in his pocket, a string cheese, and he holds it out. The little puppy sniffs and comes out of the bush. She has blood on her back leg, and she squeaks a sad squeak when she walks. She is shaking, and I don't know if she is cold or scared or both.

Momma is in the backyard, and I see her waving for us to come home. I take off my jacket, wrap her up, and carry her down the mountain.

"Momma, look!"

"Oh, poor baby. She has no collar. Let's get her inside and bathe her in the sink."

Momma says she has no fleas and her foot is cut so it is bleeding. We help Momma clean her up and wrap her foot and give her water.

Miss Suzanne, Dylan's mom, brings over some puppy food, and we make her a bed with a blanket.

Then we have to talk. Momma says we have to make signs and put them up in the neighborhood and on the hiking trails at Shadow Mountain. We make them and say: "Found Dog—Call and Describe" and our phone number. Momma writes outlines for the letters and numbers, and we all color them in.

The puppy is tired, and she goes to sleep.

In the morning, all us boys put up the signs, but I hope no one calls.

# CHAPTER 22

*December 24, 1988*

> God never gives someone a gift they are not capable of receiving. If he gives us the gift of Christmas, it is because we all have the ability to understand and receive it.
> —Pope Francis

Whether or not the puppy is an answer to prayer is up for debate, but no one called to claim her. Ethan names her Roamy, for obvious reasons. She is perfectly healthy and only about three months old. She and Ethan have bonded, and he has been surprisingly responsible with her and his fish. So much for starting small with pets. We got thirteen in one day, just two weeks ago.

Christmas Eve is my favorite night of the year. Our family gathers at my parents' house for dinner, and then we go to midnight mass.

A live Nativity in the courtyard, including a donkey, a sheep, and the newest baby in the congregation as Jesus, draws in children and adults with a childlike wonder. Mary and Joseph greet all of the children and let them come see their baby Jesus up close. Ethan and his cousins gather around the manger, admiring the baby as if he is the actual Savior in the flesh.

"Was Jesus this tiny?"

"Yes, he was a baby and a little boy just your size."

Ethan pulls glow sticks out of his pocket and lays them in the manger for baby Jesus. He turns and leads us all into church.

The church sparkles with tiny white lights and candles on the altar. Christmas trees shimmer on each side of the chancel. The choir leads Christmas carols. The sound is amplified off the walls, and joyous tunes surround us.

"And the angel said to them, 'Fear not, for behold, I bring you good tidings of great joy which shall be to all people. For unto us is born this day in the city of David a Savior which is Christ the Lord'" (Luke 2:10–11, KJV).

The lights are all turned off. We stand in silent darkness, and then as the first candle is lit, the choir sings "Silent Night." The flame is passed from one person to the next, row by row. Hundreds of little flames cast a warm glow on each of hundreds of faces, reminding us of the light of the world. Together, they light up the whole church. I feel like I'm glowing from the inside out.

When we get home, Ethan is asleep. I carry him to bed, and Roamy jumps up with him.

It is still dark outside but morning. I gave away my glow sticks last night. The aquarium lights my room now.

"It's Christmas, Momma! Get up!"

I have to wait while Momma lights up the Christmas tree and the fire. We go to the living room, and I look at the presents under the tree. We eat cinnamon rolls and read the Christmas story out of the Bible.

Roamy has a stocking, and I help her open a bone. She takes it to her cushion, and I open my stocking. After we open lots of cool presents, it is time to go to G'ma and G'pa's house.

My cousins and everybody are there. All day is super fun. Alex, Trevor, and I drive remote control cars in the street. We lie down on the green grass and see clouds of shapes. We have really good dinner, and the kids' table has everything the same as the grown-ups' table, except we have grape juice, not wine, in glasses with stems. They are fragile and special for Christmas.

When Momma and I get home, the door is not locked. Momma calls inside, and no one is there. But a bike is! Santa must have brought it while we were gone. It probably didn't fit in the chimney so he had to use the door. Momma is looking all over the house, but she finds no more gifts for her.

Outside, I ride my bike all around the cul-de-sac, and Momma watches. She has her straight-across smile, but I have a big, big smile!

# CHAPTER

*December 31, 1988*

---

Be at war with your vices, at peace with your neighbors, and let every new year find you a better man.
—Benjamin Franklin

---

On a mellow New Year's Eve, the children play in Ethan's room while we play Scrabble. We switch to Catch Phrase, and the noise level rises as we laugh and shout out answers. Music plays, and we have Times Square's New Year's Eve coverage on the TV. Mike is the only one who hears someone at the door, and he answers.

Jace stands in the doorway and calls, "Why didn't you invite me, Kate?"

"Who are you?" Mike says.

Jace blows right past him into my living room. Janet and Barry step in front of him.

"You need to go!" Barry says sternly.

Jace shoves Barry. "Hey, friend. Get outta my way. Nice job on the Christmas lights, Kate."

Gwen and her date, Geoff, go to check on the kids and distract them in the bedroom. I hear the bedroom door close.

Jace pushes his way past Barry and Janet.

Barry and Mike grab him and literally throw him out the door.

Roamy has made her way to the front porch and barks.

Jace stands, dusts himself off, and grabs the scruff of her neck. She dangles from his outstretched hand, wiggles, and yelps.

I rush at Jace. "Put her down! Stop, Jace!"

"Stay away, Kate, or I swear I'll twist her little neck!"

"She's Ethan's puppy, Jace. Let her down!"

He backs away, taking Roamy with him as I plead for her life.

"The little mutt tried to bite me!"

"That's your fault. Now, let her go!"

Mike and Barry run out the back door, round each side of the house and, through the darkness, rush him from both sides.

Roamy is yelping and trembling, and I wrap her in my arms.

"Psycho!" Janet yells.

Suzanne puts a hand on Janet's arm to shush her.

Neighbors peek out their doors and windows. I look at Ethan's bedroom window and am thankful that the blinds are closed. The music is still blaring, so the children are unaware that anything is amiss.

Mike and Barry have Jace pinned to the ground.

I take Roamy to Ethan's room.

"Is it almost midnight?" Mae says. The kids turn their attention to me.

"Almost! Just wait here while I get stuff ready. Keep Roamy in here with you."

When I get back to the living room, the guys are back inside. Jace is gone.

Everyone gathers together, and we count down as the ball drops. Confetti poppers explode, and we toast and kiss our loved ones. When we ring in the New Year, it appears that I am the only person who is worried about what could happen next.

However, Roamy is standing stock-still, facing the front door. I pick her up and scratch behind her ears, but she doesn't avert her gaze.

"Momma, what's psycho?" Ethan says.

"You know, when you play Catch Phrase and someone might say, 'This is an old movie with a crazy person, and it starts at Christmastime when the cowboy Santa wreaths are on the light posts!' And you might guess the answer: *Psycho*! That's the name of the movie. Cheers!" I tap his glass of 7-Up with my champagne, and he is satisfied with my answer for now.

# CHAPTER 24

*January 7, 1989*

---

Don't give your son money. As far as you can afford it, give him horses. No one ever came to grief except honorable grief through riding horses. No hour of life is lost that is spent in the saddle.
—Sir Winston Churchill

---

We arrive for our first time at the stables. Our instructor meets us with currycombs, brushes, and hoof picks. He's a tall, lean, muscular man in well-worn western wear and a cowboy hat that shades his pale blue eyes.

"I'm Grayson Bennett. It's nice to meetcha. Let's go on over to the corral. I have a couple of horses who need groomin'." He hands us each a set of grooming tools and grabs some bridles.

As we follow Grayson through the wide-open barn, Ethan whispers, "I thought we were gonna ride."

"You can't just jump on the horse and go. You have to be sure that he has no dirt that will cause sores under his saddle and get to know him a little bit first," I whisper back to him.

"That's true," Grayson says.

I talked to Grayson at length on the phone when I set up this lesson and found out that he is well acquainted with children like Ethan, who for a variety of reasons, cannot control their bodies or have other emotional issues. His theory is that when children have to be aware of their own movements in order to control a large animal, it transfers over to everyday life. Riding engages your core and inner thighs. You must be strong and relaxed. Riding offers many sensory stimuli as well.

"Because they are prey animals," Grayson says, "horses react more like us than a dog might. They run or kick if they are scared. Ethan, how would you feel if someone came at you fast and loud and you didn't know what he was up to?"

His question surprises Ethan. "I would not be able to move my legs."

Grayson nods. "Because you would feel afraid. That is why it is important to let the horses know you are there and what you are up to when you approach them." Grayson turns to me. "Horses mirror your mood. When Ethan is dealing with that reflection, he will be learning to manage himself."

We enter the corral, and Grayson closes the gate.

"Ethan, I want you to walk calmly up to that paint horse. He's the one you will work with today. He's very gentle, but if you startle him, he'll get scared—and we don't want that. Walk up to his side 'cause he can't see you if you come right up behind him. Say something to him so he knows you are there."

"Hey, paint horse, I came to brush you," Ethan says. Once he is close enough to touch the horse, the horse turns and rubs his muzzle on Ethan's outstretched hand. Ethan jerks his hand back quickly and squeals. The horse shakes his head, and Ethan nearly flips over himself, drops his tools, and jumps to a safe distance, looking unsure about this whole idea.

Grayson strokes the horse and says, "It's okay, Benjamin. Ethan, come and meet Benjamin Moore."

Ethan walks toward Benjamin Moore and feels his velvety

muzzle. He reaches higher to stroke his forehead, and Benjamin Moore leans down to let him feel his forelock.

"It's kinda wiry," Ethan observes.

"It is," Grayson says as he picks up a brush and hands it to Ethan. "Ya want to brush in the same direction the hair grows. Did ya ever brush a dog?"

"Yeah."

"Kate, you can brush that roan mare. Her name is Scarlett. She's a little feisty, but you can handle that, right?" Grayson says with a wide, knowing grin.

I savor the aroma of dust and horse as I brush her. I lean into her with my shoulder and grasp her fetlock, placing her hoof up on my thigh to pick out the packed dirt. As I make my way around her, I feel a sense of well-being that I haven't felt for a long time.

Grayson has Ethan brush Benjamin Moore systematically front to back. "Ya want to brush in short strokes and get rid of anything you loosened up with the currycomb. Keep a hand on his shoulder while you brush his leg. Good job."

When they finish, Grayson saddles up Benjamin Moore. He shows Ethan how to put the bit in Benjamin's mouth and slips the bridle over his head. Grayson boosts Ethan up into the saddle, and Ethan clings to the saddle horn with both hands while Grayson adjusts the stirrups. Benjamin Moore shifts his weight, and Ethan, startled, says, "Whoa!" He then giggles at himself for being scared.

With the reins in his hand, Grayson leads Benjamin Moore around the corral. Ethan relaxes into the saddle. After a couple of times around, Grayson says, "Are you ready to go by yourself? Just pull back on the reins to tell Benjamin to stop. To go, lean forward and give him a little nudge with your heels."

Ethan nods, and Grayson hands over the reins—and the control—to my little boy. Ethan smiles tentatively and grips the reins.

Grayson assures me that Benjamin Moore is his most mellow horse. He always uses him for first-time riders. He walks alongside of the horse and says, "Lean a little to the left and lay the reins over that way."

Ethan grins with pure elation. "He's doing it! He's obeying!"

"You are telling him what to do when you move your body, so be careful that you communicate the thing you want him to do," Grayson says.

I saddle my horse, tighten the cinch, mount her, and ride over to Ethan. We walk our horses around together, enjoying the rhythm of their strides. Scarlett is antsy, and I have to hold her back to keep pace with Ethan. It occurs to me that I need to hold back a little in life with Ethan and let him heal in his own time. I need to master patience.

We walk circles and figure eights, and the time flies. When we finish and dismount, Grayson takes Ethan's saddle back to the tack room and instructs him on brushing again.

As I tend to Scarlett, I watch Ethan, gentle and strong, brushing and stroking Benjamin Moore. Scarlett nudges me with her muzzle. "Sorry, girl. I was preoccupied with my son. Surely you can understand that."

Scarlett appropriately nods her head as if she understands, and I smile and stroke her velvety neck.

"Ethan, it's time to pick up the manure." Grayson approaches with a manure fork. "It wouldn't be right to leave our mess for someone else to clean up." He smiles and shows Ethan how to toss the manure into a wheelbarrow.

Ethan struggles, dropping most of his load on the ground, but he is determined to get it all into the wheelbarrow. When he finally finishes, we say our goodbyes. Our drive home is quiet as we process our experience.

# CHAPTER 25

## January 1989

---

The object of art is to give life a shape.
—Jean Anouilh, *The Rehearsal*

---

Our parent-child watercolor class is a lot of fun. I haven't painted in ages. It's at a community center, so it is very affordable. An earthy woman teaches it. Dharma is around fifty years old, wrapped in skin that looks closer to sixty. Wild, long, salt-and-pepper hair hangs to her waist, and the sunlight from the window catches glittery strands as she passes its beams. Her customary attire is a Danskin top with a gauze multicolored skirt from Star of India. On her feet, she wears hiking boots with wool socks if she's cold, and nothing if she's warm. She often experiences both body temperatures in the same class period. Her eyes light up, and she waves her arms in exaggerated brushstrokes while she explains our next project. She smiles all the time. Her ebullience is contagious.

Ethan paints my portrait in an assignment to paint your table partner. He uses his usual dark colors for most of it. He actually makes a wash of pink for my cheeks, and my mouth is the shape of a wide, upturned crescent.

"You made me so pretty, Ethan." It strikes me that he really does … make me pretty, that is. My love for him brings out the best in me, and that is my beauty.

At the end of class, Dharma stops to admire Ethan's work.

"You are coming right along, little man." She swirls a pointed finger over his painting as if her magic wand will make the smiling face true, forever. "This is exquisite."

Ethan beams and says, "I tried a new color. Pink. Because Momma isn't gray any more."

"I'm glad to hear that, sir." Dharma uses various pronouns when talking to her students. It ensures that she won't call someone the wrong name. "Being happy is a choice. I had to try very hard to be happy after I was gray for a time."

"Why were you gray?" Ethan pries as only a child can.

"Ethan," she actually says his name, and he takes notice, "my momma and daddy died, and it made me very sad. They were not old, but the choices they made in their lives caused them leave this earth prematurely. That was the tragic consequence. You know what a consequence is, right?"

"Yes, o'course," Ethan says.

"I had to make choices about my life, and I choose to be happy and productive and to experience all that life has to offer me now, right in this moment and every moment. At times, something happens that makes me feel sad or scared, but once it's over, I choose to enjoy the moment I am experiencing. Would you like to work with some clay?"

"Like Play-Doh? Yes! I make lots of stuff with Play-Doh. I tried drying one, but it got crusty. Now I just put it back in the plastic when I am done," Ethan chatters as he follows Dharma across the room. Dharma sets Ethan up on the far end of the classroom with a lump of clay and various tools. She sticks her thumbs in deep and pinches a hole in the clay to get him started. "You have to make a hole inside like that or it won't turn out. If you work hard and make something you like, I'll fire it for you in the kiln. Then it will last for your whole life."

As I gather my things, Dharma approaches. "Kate, I don't know what you are going through ... except that you mentioned a restraining order."

"It's been hard, but I think things are on the upswing. I feel so bad for failing Ethan for so long."

"Ethan is a strong little boy. He'll be okay. You know that's the meaning of his name, don't you? Strong, firm."

I nod, yes.

Dharma continues, "And you are Katherine?"

"Kathleen."

"Okay, the Irish form. Same name. Pure. That is you, pure as the driven snow. As gold, refined. You might consider living as if that is who you are. A name is an important thing. It can describe who you were or who you are, like the names in the Bible. A barren woman pleads with God for a baby, and he grants her a son. She names him Samuel—God hears. That's just one example."

I smile and say with the boldness of my child, "What's the meaning of Dharma?"

"Ha-ha-ha." She laughs. "That describes who I used to be. I keep it to remind me. It keeps me centered. And nobody ever says, 'Which Dharma are you referring to?' So, that's a convenience. Dharma would take some time to explain. It's been used in various ways in Hindu and Buddhist thought for millennia. It has multiple translations, but it means little in Western culture. In Hinduism, dharma enables a person to satisfy the striving for stability and order, a life that is lawful and harmonious, the striving to do the right thing, be good, be virtuous, earn religious merit, be helpful to others, interact successfully with society. All that perfection seems like a lot of work to me. My parents wanted me to start at the top, I suppose, so they named me for the best they could offer. You can't truly give your child what you don't possess yourself. Honestly, I think they were smoking something when they came up with it. It made sense, where they were in life. It was a good gift that they gave me from their hearts. But God, the true God, gives better. Here's the thing, as a Christian, because of Jesus, Dharma is just a vague memory in many ways. It reminds me of where I came from, but dharma can't give the peace that Jesus does. Dharma doesn't make one free."

She doesn't look or dress like any Christian I have seen, but she is free, I'll grant her that. Maybe you don't have to fit a mold to be a follower of Christ. I try to wrap my mind around what she said when Ethan says from across the room, "You could change it. I had a caterpillar named Pilar, and when he turned into a butterfly, he became so beautiful that I named him Pattern."

"Ha-ha-ha." Dharma laughs, waves her arms and folds herself in half with glee, whooshing her shirt across her knee with her hand, as if the hand is traveling on its own. "I could indeed, Ethan. But I'd hate to think what name would best describe me! Maybe Wrinkles or Silly?"

"Maybe Joy," Ethan says.

"Maybe Joy," Dharma says in a hushed tone that I hadn't heard from her before. She smiles and walks over to see what Ethan has made.

"It's me and Momma. I made it from just one lump of clay because that's how much she loves me—and I love her."

We are each a cone shape, him small and me bigger, joined into one cone base. Each cone is rounded on the top. He's carved a smile for each of us and made my curly hair with the wire loop on one of his tools. My hands are disproportionally large, and they envelop his little body, which blends with mine.

"Oh, Ethan. That is lovely! I will fire it and give it to you next week to glaze."

Ethan is so excited he can hardly stand it. So am I.

# CHAPTER 26

## February 1989

---

That which does not kill us makes us stronger.
—Friedrich Nietzsche

---

Roamy barks to say that someone is at the door.
"Kathleen Evans?" the man inquires.
"Yes?"
"You've been served."
"What?"
"This is an order to appear. You can read it."
He turns and leaves me standing with an envelope in my hand, shaking as if he is Jace in the flesh.

When Suzanne arrives to pick up Dylan, I show her the summons. "Wow!" is all she can muster.

Ethan, Carson, and Dylan are playing out back. Gwen is sitting at my kitchen table. She has been through this sort of thing before, twice, once with Carson's dad and once with her three-year-old Monique's dad. She's a helpful sounding board.

"I think I need a lawyer. Do you think? What do you think? Is it worth the money? I know what this is about. He wants

Ethan—maybe not all the time—but he wants him." I suck in air and rub my head with both hands. I need to think.

"Let's be calm. We can work through this together." Gwen's quiet, Southern voice lulls me like a lullaby.

The boys come to the door for Kool-Aid. Gwen says, "Y'all go get a drink from the hose. We'll holler when it's time to come in. Now go on." You don't have to tell those boys twice to go play with the hose, and they are gone.

"You've kept a journal, like I told you, right? Dates and precise details of events will help. Jace can lie under oath if he wants to, but your written details make it harder. With those notes you won't get so flustered when you are questioned. You'll have it all laid out in front of you. Bank statements are necessary."

"Wait, what? Why? He wants Ethan, not money!" *Get a grip*, I tell myself.

"Dawlin', you have to be prepared for anything he might throw in your court, pun intended."

I get the journal from my nightstand, and she looks it over with approval while I fix some Kool-Aid and a plate of apple wedges and peanut butter, my standby, waterproof snack. I run the snack out to the dripping, shirtless boys.

She finishes skimming my journal. "This is great. You even went back to the beginnin' to show the pattern of abuse. You know, you are a strong person to have worked so hard and stayed so long."

"I never thought I was strong. I thought it was a weakness, my own sickness."

"No," she says firmly. "Look at all this time between abuses when you thought things were okay and thought that he had changed. You camped, went to the beach, barbequed with friends. You made pottery together. How many people can say that they made their own dishes and the beer in their mugs? Those were good and fun times, right?"

I nod, and Gwen continues. "People tend to think that life will always be as it is in the present. If we are flat broke, we think we will always be broke. If we are rich or happy or busy, we think it will always be. You had good times and bad, like everyone does. You just had to live long enough to identify the pattern in order to know the cycle would continue. You had to be sure before you ended your marriage. Sure, looking back you can say, 'I shoulda' left the first time he hit me, or before that, the first time he was rude to me.' Don't beat yourself up over it, dawlin'. We don't have the advantage of experience in the beginnin'."

And Suzanne says, "Wow."

Later that night, cozy in my bed, my heart pounds. My mind races. My stomach churns. I feel terror before my thoughts are fully formed. I remember times long past and try to convince myself that the memories cannot hurt me. I try to focus on good times—the ones Gwen mentioned, camping and the beauty of the Rockies and barbeques—but my mind is persistent. Every memory leads me to a dark place, a party gone bad or wandering streets alone at night in a strange town, looking for help.

Do you know the dream where you can't get away because your feet are stuck and your voice doesn't work when you try to scream? That's what my life was like back then. I'd escape from a beating and walk into a shop, but I couldn't speak. I'd ask for a phone book instead of saying, "My husband is after me. He's beating me, and I need to get away. Can I hide here until I can get some help?"

Then Jace would drive up, and I'd get back in the car because I had no words to explain to a stranger why I needed a bus ticket back to California or a place to stay for the night. In my mind, I'd foresee the scenario; telling the stranger that I was in danger, law enforcement involvement, his parents and my parents and all of our friends clamoring around us. It was easier to just get back into the car. Jace told me he wouldn't hit me if I didn't make him so mad. I guess in the short term that was easier to deal with than all of those other people.

Dr. Quist says that it is likely that Jace will treat his child the same way he treated me, eventually, but the courts don't make orders based on what might happen, statistically speaking, in the future. An abusive incident involving the child has to have happened already or be a current threat. That means that I could be ordered to send Ethan away with Jace on Wednesday nights and every other weekend. If I don't let him go, I will be in contempt of court. My head starts to pound, and I am sweating. I run to the bathroom and throw up in the toilet.

# CHAPTER 27

*April 1989*

---

> You gain strength, courage, and confidence by every experience in which you really stop to look fear in the face. You must do the thing which you think you cannot do.
> —Eleanor Roosevelt

---

The hearings take place, and each focuses on one issue: battery, custody and visitation, and child support. Regarding the issue of domestic violence, Jace is ordered to go through a domestic violence program, and he receives a figurative wrist slap.

The custody and visitation hearing is my biggest concern. As I drive downtown, I pray that the judge will be fair and that the truth would be told. I am armed with my journal recording dates and details of abuses, Ethan's trouble at school, his fears and nightmares. I have samples of his dark artwork.

We are sworn in, and each of us has a chance to speak. Jace says he wants Ethan half of the time. The judge says that it is customary for the parent receiving the child to pick him up. Jace wants me to drive Ethan to him and needs me to pick him up after the visit.

I mention his pattern of abuse. The judge says he cannot rule based on a presumption that something may happen in the future. He understands my concern, but Jace has not physically abused Ethan, and we can't prove that Ethan's fears or misbehavior stem from his early childhood trauma.

I fear that Jace will be awarded shared custody and half of Ethan's life with him, and I mention Jace's drinking as a safety concern.

Jace says, "That's why you have to bring him to me and pick him up. I am not driving."

The judge asks Jace why he is not driving.

Jace buries himself without me having to say a word. "Because my license is revoked, and every time I get pulled over for DUI, they add on more years!"

The judge's poker face cracks a smile, and he says he's heard enough. He orders supervised visits at Jace's expense, every other Wednesday, for two hours.

As we leave the courthouse, Jace says to me in a nasty tone, "Well, you got what you wanted."

"Not everything," I say. I turn and leave him as he heads to the bus stop.

It's sad to see how life has left him defeated. If I had gotten what I wanted, it would have been a long time ago—and we would be happy together as a family. I suppose he didn't even know what a happy family looked like. If only his parents had known what went on in the mind of their child, the pain and rage, the feeling of having no control, he could have been something great.

# CHAPTER 28

*April 1989*

---

> You always had the power, my dear, you just had to learn it for yourself.
> —Glinda, *The Wizard of Oz*

---

"You be Racer, Dylan, 'cause you are the fastest horse who ever lived. Carson is Buck like in Bonanza. I am Silver, and I have a silver sword."

"You can't have a sword, Ethan. You don't have hands," Carson says.

"Well, we are horses what talk, so why not a sword? I can hold it in my teeth."

"That's just dumb," Dylan says.

"All right," I say. "But I am faithful and brave."

We lope all over the desert and play that we guard the western town from bad guys who want to come in and steal and kill. We run and rear up on our hind legs, and we stop them before they can burn down the farmer's barn. Everyone in the town has a parade for us and gives us a feast. We have Funyons, apples, and baby carrots, and we drink from the hose like it is a waterfall. Then we rest under the trees.

I think that I wish I was a real protector. Momma says that I am, from the time my dad broke in the window and I called 911. Carson has a dad who lives away, but he is good to Carson and Miss Gwen. Carson gets to go on visits with him. That's what I wish too.

"Eww! What's that smell?" Dylan says as he comes to retrieve his lunchbox for a Funyon feast. The boys are playing "wild horses." These wild horses love Funyons, and I, "Momma Horse," give them a bucketful of apples and baby carrots to round out their horsey diet.

Gwen and I are giving each other perms, and the ammonia smell fills the house. I have finished rolling hers, and the solution is doing its magic on Gwen's hair as she rolls mine.

"Leave that door open when you go out, Dylan," Gwen says as she wraps another pink perm rod with paper and a strand of my hair.

"Why you do dat?" Monique says as she plays with the pile of rollers.

"So that our hair will be as pretty as yours," Gwen says. Monique grins and shakes her dark cornrows, clicking colorful beads together. Gwen turns back to our conversation. "Would y'all like to go out for pizza when we're done with this? If I try to make dinner this late, it'll be eight o'clock by the time it's done. Stuart's coming over when he gets off work, so I have plenty of time."

"Yes, that would be great. Suzanne said Mike's gone tonight, so she'll probably join us. Who's Stuart? What happened to Geoff? Oh, never mind."

"Monique, hand me another roller, dawlin'. Thank you. You're such a helper! So, Kate, tell me all about court."

"Not much to tell. He gets supervised visits, twice a month for two hours on Wednesdays. That's it. Thank you, Gwen, for your encouragement. I felt much calmer going in because I was prepared—thanks to you."

"Naw. You were ready all along. You just didn't know it," Gwen says.

When our hair is processed, washed, and dried, and our bangs are teased up high, we think we look presentable enough to go to Pizza Hut. Suzanne and Dylan join us for dinner. We celebrate my new life, newfound strength, and confidence.

# CHAPTER 26

*May 3, 1989*

---

Learn this from me. Holding anger is a poison. It eats you from inside. We think that hating is a weapon that attacks the person who harmed us. But hatred is a curved blade. And the harm we do, we do to ourselves.
—Mitch Albom, *The Five People You Meet in Heaven*

---

Ethan and I arrive at Jace's first court-ordered, supervised visit promptly and go into the facility where the visit is to take place. "There's like a house in here." Ethan takes a seat on the couch for about a second. When he spots the toys, he crosses the room to look into the collection.

A freckled woman with a gap between her two front teeth and a wide smile shows him where to get Play-Doh, crayons and paper, toys, and books. He walks right past the play kitchen and selects Lincoln Logs with which he is fully engaged when Jace arrives, late. I smell stale liquor on his breath as he passes me with a smug expression. The woman with the gap between her teeth takes a seat, and I realize that she will be the one to stay to monitor the visit. I am escorted to a waiting area where I absentmindedly flip through magazines, waiting for the two-hour visitation to be over.

I don't hate Jace. He looks tired and worn down. Alcohol and living hard have faded his striking good looks. I feel bad for him. I probably look worn down to him too. I suddenly feel exhausted. I close my magazine and my eyes. My anger is justifiable, but bitterness will take its toll on me. I say a quick silent prayer that bitterness will not grow in my heart. My anger keeps me alert. It is more of a passion to keep Ethan safe than anger targeted at Jace. Mixed-up thoughts and emotions swirl in my head as I doze off.

Ethan's shouts jolt me awake. I hurry to the reception desk where a birdlike woman looks over her glasses at me. I ask if I can go back to the family room.

She says, "The child psychologist on duty will manage and deescalate the situation. It is not unusual for the children to have a hard time adapting to their new surroundings."

"It's not the surroundings that he is yelling about. I need to check on him." I plead with the bird woman, but she pushes her glasses up her beaklike nose and looks down at her papers still talking to me, disinterestedly. "I'm sorry ma'am, but it is his father's visitation time, so you can't—"

A man with authority, and a pocket protector below his nametag, interrupts her. "Mrs. Evans? Please come this way." The child psychologist leads me back to the family room.

The Lincoln Log house is scattered, and the play kitchen is knocked over. Ethan sobs and thrashes around while the freckled, gap-toothed woman physically restrains him for his own protection. I detect relief in her expression as I approach. Ethan is completely out of control.

Jace is sitting in the corner, head in his hands. He looks up as I enter the room, and the sorrow on his face is tragic.

The child psychologist has joined the woman with Ethan and is trying to redirect my son, but it's not working. I grab a throw blanket off of the couch, walk over to Ethan, and swaddle him like a baby. It's what I do when he loses control at home. I wrap him up tight, pick him up, and take him to a rocking chair. We rock and rock, and he cries until he is completely exhausted. The two workers speak to each other in hushed tones, and the freckled, gap-toothed woman has lost her smile to a look of concern.

Ethan's gone limp in my arms, his hair wet with sweat.

Jace says, "See what you've done? You turned him against me." His daggers always pierce me deeply, especially when I know it isn't true.

The two staff members hustle Jace out the door, and we are left in the quiet.

My dad is gone, and I am glad. I want to see him, but I don't at the same time. I kicked the Lincoln Logs and knocked over the play kitchen. That was breaking rule 3. Respect all property. My angry is out!

Momma wraps me in a blanket, and I feel safe—like Pilar in his cocoon. Black Beauty's mom would not like it if he behaved like I did. My mom is not happy about it either, but I know she still loves me while we rock.

I come out of my cocoon, I feel tears again. I don't look at anyone. Momma holds my hand tight, and we leave that place.

# CHAPTER

*May 4, 1989*

---

> Bad things do happen; how I respond to them defines my character and the quality of my life. I can choose to sit in perpetual sadness, immobilized by the gravity of my loss or I can choose to rise from the pain and treasure the most precious gift I have—life itself.
> —Walter Anderson

---

In the morning, I consider keeping Ethan home from school. Froot Loops on his Cheerios don't even lift his gloomy mood. He is resistant to going, but I tell him that we all have our responsibilities. He is going to school, and I am going to work. I slip a Ninja Turtle Pez into his snack bag.

"See you later, alligator." I smile and give him a pinkie hug at his classroom door.

"After a while, crocodile," he moans, sounding something like Eeyore.

When I arrive at Tattered Treasures, Mrs. Leoni greets me with her usual, lighthearted, "Buona mattina, bellissima! Coffee is ready in the back."

"Thank you, Mrs. Leoni."

I must have my straight across smile on my face because she follows me into the back room and asks, "What is the matter?"

I tell her all about Ethan's visitation with Jace, and when I finish, she says, "Well, that's over. Enjoy your coffee, bella." She leaves the room to the sound of the door chimes and adds, "Enjoy your new day!"

I tag the new arrivals in the back of the store and set aside some pants for Ethan. Customers have animated conversations with Mrs. Leoni. Their joyous laughter blows into the back room, parting the gloom that I feel. I ponder their joy, so contradictory to what I am going through. It is like when someone you love dies, and you are completely absorbed in your own grief and plans. It is strange that the rest of the world goes on as if nothing has happened. I suppose I can choose to join them in their happiness, but instead, I feel sorry for myself for a little while longer.

We sit down for lunch together, and Mrs. Leoni says, "Katie, you know that woman who was just here?"

"Yes, Mrs. Stepanovych. She's really sweet," I reply. She shops here frequently and always spreads her cheer.

"Yes, Natasha Stepanovych. Let me tell you what I know. This is not gossip. It's history. You can confirm it with Natasha if you'd like. She won't mind. When Natasha was a young woman in Ukraine, she had no husband. She walked to church across town in the snow with holes in her shoes. She stood in the church service for hours because the more prominent families used the pews. One Sunday, a kind woman invited Natasha to join her family in their private pew. This kind woman and her husband had two boys. The little one was strong and active. The older one was crippled from birth and could not walk. That little crippled boy was sweet as the day is long. He grew very fond of Natasha.

"Then, one day, the woman's family was not in church. Natasha sat alone in the pew for the whole service. When it was over, the priest came to her to tell her that the kind woman had died. She had been sick for a long time and had never mentioned it to Natasha.

The priest went on to say that the woman had chosen Natasha to marry her husband and raise her children when she died. She had to provide a mother for her crippled son.

"Natasha did marry that man, and she is married to him still. She will tell you that she married for the love of the children and not for love of the man. In their village, Natasha walked miles with that little boy on her back to take him to the park. She loved those children, and eventually had some babies of her own.

"When the Nazis came to her village, they murdered everybody they could. She will tell you, 'Murder, murder, murder!' She and the children hid, and their lives were spared, but the next time the Nazis came, that sweet crippled boy who was now a young man of eighteen, said to Natasha, 'Take the younger children and go. You must. I cannot go with you as we would all surely die.' She never saw that son again.

"Katie, we all have things in our lives that are hard, and some are harder than others. Our own attitude and response make some situations worse. You can choose to let things weigh you down—or you can choose to be thankful for what you have. You, Bella, have Ethan, and a wonderful family. Choose your focus. It will define you."

# CHAPTER 31

*June 1989*

---

> How wonderful it is that nobody need wait a single moment before starting to improve the world.
> —Anne Frank

---

Saturday mornings have been a highlight each week. Riding has become a passion for Ethan as it was for me as a girl. I love sharing the experience with him.

"He's a natural," Grayson says.

The time has finally arrived to leave the corral and take a trail ride. Ethan chatters in excited anticipation all the way out to the ranch. We pull into the driveway between a pair of large wooden posts and head to the barn. An abrupt scream comes from the back seat of my car as soon as we pass through the gate. Ethan completely loses it. He cries inconsolably.

"What is wrong, Ethan?" I turn off the ignition.

"I don't want to! It's dumb, and I don't want to go! Let's go home!"

I am caught completely off guard. He's been waiting for this for weeks. He got all ramped up and then had a complete meltdown.

"Ethan, stop." I don't know what to do with him. I see Grayson near the barn, and he waves.

"Listen, Ethan. Grayson is waiting for us, and we need to go."

"No!" he wails.

"It is time, and I am going." I take the keys and walk away, leaving the car doors open.

"Good morning, Grayson." I walk toward the barn.

Seeing Ethan, Grayson says, "I have an idea." He walks off to the house. A few minutes later, he comes back with a box full of paints, brushes of various sizes, well-used palettes and cups of water. He heads to the stalls without a word, and I follow, curious. "We are going to paint them," he says matter-of-factly. We lead three horses to the corral, tie them up, and brush them clean. Ethan watches from the car. We squeeze tempera paints onto the palettes. "Avoid the areas where the saddle blankets and cinch will be," Grayson says. Then he confidently paints his horse with designs fit for a parade. The horse loves the gentle stroking, shakes his withers, and swishes a fly away with his tail. They certainly are sensitive creatures to be able to notice when a fly lands on them. My paint job is not nearly as intricate, but Scarlett loves how the paintbrush feels.

Ethan emerges from the car and trudges toward us, kicking a stone, stopping to look at something on the ground, and poking it with a stick. He slowly edges his way over to the corral and rests his chin on the fence, curious but silent. Eventually, he picks up a currycomb and grooming brush and brushes Benjamin Moore until he shines. He collects paint bottles, a brush, and a palette. On the white part of Benjamin's right side, he paints an angry face in dark blue.

He walks around to the other side of his horse, petting him and quietly says, "Sorry, Benjamin Moore."

I can see Ethan's bottom half on the other side of his horse as I finish painting a swirl on Scarlett's forehead.

I rinse off my paintbrush and walk around to the other side

of Benjamin Moore. Ethan painted a bright yellow happy face on a dark patch of Benjamin's coat. Then he puts his fingers in the paints, and streaks them across his face like war paint, yellow, blue, red, green, and watery black, like the mixed emotions that clash to his core.

We box up the paints, and I saddle up for our trail ride. I marvel at the way Grayson simply, seemingly without effort, makes the world a better place. Grayson helps Ethan mount up and gives him a quick review in the corral. When Ethan is comfortable, Grayson mounts his horse and opens the gate.

Clop, clop, clop, clop, clop, clop. That's what I hear. Momma and Grayson are on each side of me. The desert looks deadish, but it is actually alive. It has Joshua trees with arms up and sprawly, and cactus what you can make jelly out of, or drink from, if you are dying out there. Grayson shows us an oasis of palm trees, like a million of them, or maybe thousand. They are an army of giants with long, brown, feathery tunics and green sprouts on top of their heads, not like the trimmed-up naked ones in town. They guard us and keep us safe. I imagine masked bandits come to take our gold from in our saddlebags. I have war paint so they know they better not come here. The bandits stay up in the hills, hidden behind rocks. The palm tree army is too big for them to fight, like a million Goliaths. I see their dust as they ride away.

"Oh, look, Ethan, cute baby quails with their momma!" Momma says. She's talking about the scenery and cute little birds. She sees a different desert than I see. Hers is pretty, but mine is safe.

"Ethan, do you want to go a little faster?" Grayson says. I get to choose, but I don't know. If I go faster, I might be in danger. I like how it is right now.

"If you do, we will stay right with you, and you can stop any time. Just pull back on the reins," Grayson says.

I think it sounds okay, so I nod.

"Just lean a little forward, give him looser reins, and nudge him in the sides with your heels," Grayson says.

"Whaaaa!" Bump, bump, bump, bump, bump goes Benjamin Moore.

"Heels down, Ethan. Thataway! Lean a little more forward and nudge him again."

When I do that, the bumping stops and he lopes, smoothly, like the wheels on my bike, but a little like Wonder Horse. The wind is blowing my face, my war paint, and my hair. I count to fifty, two times, and then we stop in the shade of big rocks and look down at the palm tree oasis. We laugh and laugh because that was so fun. Momma wants to go some more. Grayson and I watch, and I think she is like Black Beauty when he is free in the end. After all that hard life, Black Beauty gets to be back in a pasture again.

Our horses walk back and get a big drink at the stables. We get to wash them, and the paint drips onto the dirt. I wash my angry away and my happy. Grayson gets me wet with the hose, and my war paint mixes with Benjamin's paint in the dirt. I laugh and laugh, and I stomp my boots in the colors and mud.

All the way home, I talk and talk about horses and bandits and going fast and slow, and I like it all.

# CHAPTER 32

June 1989

> Art enables us to find ourselves and lose ourselves at the same time.
> —Thomas Merton

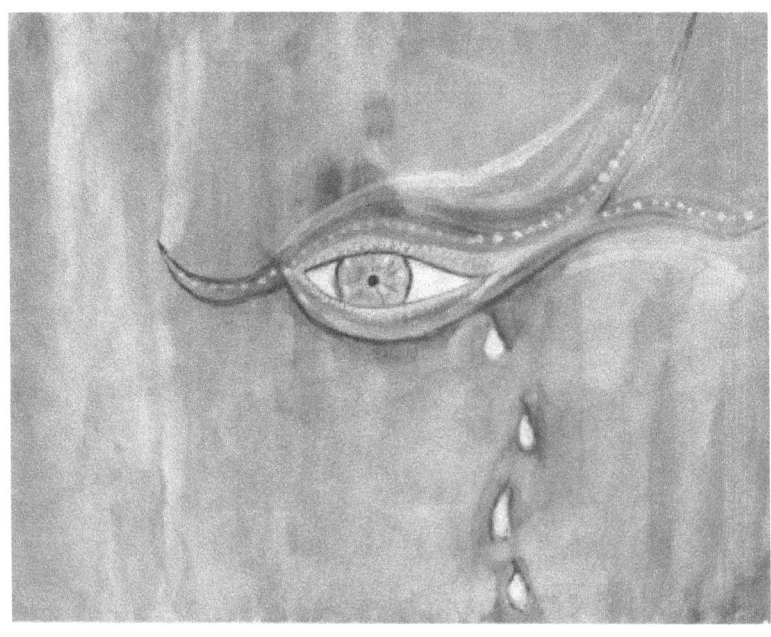

Dharma's assignment for the class today is to paint emotions without a particular subject. Our classmates produce a stunning array of abstract pieces. One is Calm with sky blue and aqua washed over the paper. In Happy, vibrant colors in geometric shapes dance across the page. Ethan's is Angry with black, gray, and brown swirls with red eyes that follow you from every angle.

Mine is Heartache. Gray-blue and purple run like tears down the page, and a blue-green eye pierces through the darkness. Without looking at each other's paintings while we work, our compositions turn out eerily similar.

We take a break to allow our paintings to dry. The negativity in our artwork embarrasses me. Art has a way of pulling out what is in the forefront of our minds.

"Rough day?" a classmate with a little girl in tow says to me.

"Rough? Yes," I say, stopping short of the whole sorry saga.

After the paintings dry, we are given pencils and Sharpies to finish the work. Dharma says to finish the page with subjects in the foreground. We discuss what that means with our children. When our artwork is finished, children with kites frolic in Happy. A woman floats on a raft in Calm. A silhouette of a downturned face barely peeks out from behind long strands of hair on Heartache.

Ethan's Angry is dark with his trademark swirling-tornado-person, arms outstretched and giant hands reaching for the red eyes.

I thought this art class would be good for us, but maybe I am wrong.

After class, Dharma brings Ethan's cone-shaped sculpture of us to our table. It is ready to glaze. She takes him to the ceramics table and lets him choose. To my astonishment, he chooses white. He paints us some green eyes and brown hair. Mine flows down my back and drips to the floor. Once fired, the white will give us adjoining crackled gowns. It really is lovely.

"Momma, I made us cracked because we are not fixed yet, but we are together, right?"

"Right."

Dharma gasps, and slaps her hands to her face. "Do Lord! I can't wait for you to have that displayed in your house! Maybe on the mantel. Do you have a mantel?"

Ethan grins and says, "Yes. That's where I think it will go."

"Well, I'll fire the glaze, and next time I see you, you can wrap it up and take it home. It is a treasure!"

"Thank you, Miss Dharma!" Ethan jumps from his stool and gives her a hug.

She hugs him back and laughs. "Thank heaven for little boys like you, Ethan!"

And just like that, *snap*, I know the art class is good for us.

We hang our paintings on the fridge and look at them for a full minute.

Ethan gets out some leftover taco fixings.

"Perfect idea." I load the taco shells with the last of the ingredients, and Ethan shakes on the Trappey's hot sauce. We take them out to the back patio to eat.

"I hear someone at the door. I'll be right back." I leave Ethan with his taco and walk inside. The blood drains from my face when I see Jace through the window. I drop my plate into the kitchen sink.

"Kate!" He pounds on the door. "Let me in."

"No, Jace. You are in violation of your restraining order. I'll call the police!"

"Katie Schmatie. Restraining order, reschmaiming order!"

*Oh, God, help me. He's wasted.*

He pounds on the door again. I run to Ethan and grab his wrist, knocking his taco to the ground. "Go to hide-and-seek cabinet—and don't come out until I tell you." I open the cabinet, grab the phone receiver from the wall, and hand it to Ethan, stretching the cord to reach. "Call 911."

I run to the bedroom closet. With shaky hands, I open the gun safe and grab my twelve-gauge shotgun. Jace pounds on the door. I click off the safety, raise the stock to my shoulder, and walk toward the entryway.

"Jace, I am armed—and I won't hesitate if you come in! So go away! Please go away! Please!"

He pounds on the door. "Really, Kate? Would you shoot me? I don't think so."

He rattles the handle, but it is locked—and so is the dead bolt. I lower the gun, but I keep it pointed toward the door. I don't know if I would shoot him. When does the situation cross over to a matter of life and death? At times, I thought I was going to die by his hands, and I didn't.

"Go away!" Time passes in slow motion. Roamy is by my side, barking, scampering in tiny circles. Her ears go back, and she turns toward the window.

Jace peers through the window, and I raise my weapon again.

"You look real tough, Kate."

I am trembling and don't know when I took my last breath. I shake out my trigger hand and reposition it, ready. "Jace, you need to go!"

"But, Katie, I love you. Let me in ... please. I don't mean any harm. I just want to see you."

Motionless, I wait.

He knocks down a hanging plant, and then another.

"Go! Please go!"

He smashes the third hanging plant through the window. I scream and deliberately fire a shot at the wall. He sprints across the yard and disappears down the street. I lean on the wall and slide down to the floor, the sound of my heartbeat louder than the distant siren. I set my shotgun in the entry closet out of sight, still accessible.

The police arrive, and I open the door for them.

"Another team has spotted him and are currently making an arrest," the male officer says.

I nod and wipe my nose on my bare arm. "Ethan, you can come out now," I call.

Ethan looks older than the boy I last saw on my patio. He is settled, calm. "I called the police, and I remembered our address this time."

"Wow, that's great, honey." I give him a hug, still shaky.

They take my statement, and with Jace in custody, I am free to resume my evening. But the thought of it all is paralyzing. I call my parents' house.

"Hi, Dad. Are you busy?" My voice quivers, and I try not to cry as I speak. "Jace was here."

"Are you okay? Where's Ethan? What—"

"We are okay. I had to get out my gun. I don't know what I would have done if he came at me, but he stayed on the porch. Dad ... I shot the wall, and he broke the window. When is he going to leave me alone?"

"I'll be right over."

"He's been arrested. You don't need to come tonight, but can you help me with the repairs in the morning?" My muscles feel like Jell-O.

Mom overhears the conversation and picks up the extension. "Kate, are you all right?"

"Yes, Mom. Maybe we will come over to your house instead." My chin quivers, and I steady my voice. "Can we sleep there?"

"Of course. Come now. I'll hold dinner for you," Mom says.

Dad says, "I'll come get you so that I can see what we need to pick up for the repairs."

"Thanks. Thank you." I don't know what I would do without them.

Ethan is back on the patio, lying on the lounge chair with his face hanging over the end. He studies a parade of ants as they carry away a taco feast.

"Well, I guess this turned out good for them," Ethan jokes.

I turn on my flashlight in hide-and-seek cabinet. I hear Dad, and I wish him to go away.

"911, what is your emergency?" a lady says.

"I am Ethan Evans at 111 Sandpiper Street. Somebody, my dad, is trying to get in, and Momma said him to go away, but he won't!"

"What is your dad's name?" she says.

"Jace Evans."

"Officers are on their way. Ethan, stay on the phone with me, okay?"

"Okay."

"Where are you, Ethan?"

"Hide-and-seek cabinet."

"Can you see out?"

"No."

"Keep the cabinet closed, okay?"

"Okay." I say 'cause o'course I will.

"Do you hear your momma?"

"Yes. She is yelling him to go away. Roamy is barking."

"I can hear Roamy. Is that your dog?"

"Yes, my pup...Oh no! The glass is break!"

"Stay in the cabinet, Ethan."

"He might come in!" Then a loud boom. "Aahhh! A shot! A shot!"

"Stay where you are, Ethan! Do you hear a siren?"

"No, no. I don't hear anything! Nothing is noise! Momma? Momma?"

"Ethan, can you hear a siren?"

"Yes, now."

"The police are almost there."

"Okay."

"You are very brave, Ethan. You are doing everything right."

I cry now, and I think maybe Momma is died. I am scared, and I shake all over.

"Ethan, are you still in the hide-and-seek cabinet?"

"Yes. I don't hear anyone. Momma might be died ... I hear now a man voice ... and Momma."

"Ethan, take a deep breath."

"Okay." I do.

"And another."

I do again.

"Ethan, you can come out now!" I hear Momma say.

The 911 lady on the phone says, "Ethan, the police are there with you now. You can do what your momma says. You did a very good job."

I go out and leave the phone on the floor 'cause I can't reach to hang up on the wall. I tell Momma what I did. And she says, "That's great." She is shaking when she hugs me, but I am not shaking now.

# CHAPTER 33

*June 1989*

---

> How does one know if she has forgiven? You tend to feel sorrow over the circumstance instead of rage. You tend to feel sorry for the person rather than angry with him. You tend to have nothing left to say about it all.
> —Clarissa Pinkola Estes

---

The idea struck me as we unloaded groceries and set them in the kitchen. "Let's have a campfire in our fire pit. We can roast marshmallows."

"Really, Mom?" Ethan looked as if he didn't believe me.

"It'll be great! Why are you calling me Mom? I'm Momma until you are at least ten, mister! Go get some roasting sticks out of the tree, and I'll get the marshmallows and firewood."

Down in the wash behind our yard is a sandy, dry riverbed. Last summer, we made a big ring of rocks in the sand for a fire pit. We have a fallen tree trunk to sit on. Ethan dubbed it "Sitting Log." Dylan and Carson spent the night recently, and we made hot dogs out there, and s'mores for dessert. There is plenty of dry wood in the wash, and we still have a pile from our last campfire.

Ethan sets twigs in a loose pile and then bigger pieces on top.

I light the fire, and he dances around it as if to make it grow. We get bigger pieces and then some split logs and make the fire roar. We park ourselves close together on Sitting Log and talk, watch the fire, and look at the stars until the flames die down. The red embers are now perfect for roasting our marshmallows. My canvas tote is packed with all of the ingredients for s'mores. At the bottom of the bag is my painting from art class. It feels as if our class was ages ago, but it was just yesterday.

We roast our marshmallows to a perfect golden brown; melted chocolate and crumbs stick to our lips.

"Mom, I mean Momma, what are you doing with that?" Ethan spots the painting at the bottom of my tote.

"I am going to burn mine. It's all of my anger and sadness in one dark painting. I've been so sad about things, about your dad, and not getting you away fast enough. I loved him, you know. I still do, but in a different way. Life got so crazy, and I am sorry you had to be a part of it. But that is all over, Ethan. Today is a new day. We will take what comes and deal with it." I stand on top of Sitting Log. "I now proclaim that my anger is hereby over!" I yell so that the stars can hear.

I jump from Sitting Log and ceremoniously lay the painting on the red embers. The middle of the painting catches fire first. The burn travels in a widening circle; brown and red eat it up until the last corner is nothing but pale ash.

I sigh, sit back down on Sitting Log, and wrap my arm around Ethan.

He peels my arm off of his shoulder and runs up the embankment of the wash, across the yard to the house.

"What are you doing?" I call, but he doesn't stop.

I stare at the embers and poke them with my stick. Little flames find their way along a fresh bit of log. The smoke from my painting has dissipated, and I look up to see stars flickering against an inky sky. They seem to affirm that my message has been received. I am rapt with contentment. Joy washes through me like water.

"I'm back. Did you miss me?" Ethan says.

"Yes. Where'd you go?"

"I got my angry watercolor painting to burn it too."

He climbs up onto Sitting Log, stands up tall, and holds his painting above his head. He shouts, "I hereby proclaim that my angry is no more!"

He jumps to the ground and puts one corner of his painting into a tiny flame. He holds it up, turns it so the flame catches all of the edge, and drops it into the fire. The whoosh as it catches fire makes him smile, as if he has been released from a restraint that would not let him move.

He's perched on Sitting Log so that our bodies touch, his feet tucked under him as if he might push off and take flight. I wrap my arm around his little body. We stare into the embers. Tiny swirls of smoke blow away in the soft breeze.

"Ethan, this is what forgiveness is." I kiss him on the head as he untucks his feet and sits, relaxed. We watch until every last ashen memory of our art disappears.

When forgiveness moves from determined words spoken with the mouth to the heart of the speaker, peace comes. Maybe not all at once, but the weight of blame and anger is lifted. For the first time in ages, I sleep like a rock. I dream good dreams, and my soul is refreshed.

I've fought for Jace, fought with him, fought against him. I've grieved, worked through the anger, and forgiven. Now that chapter in my life is over. I finally feel content with where I am, in my family with my son. I feel whole and have hope again for our future. I harbor no ill feelings for Jace and wish only the best for him, but that is his choice.

Momma and I have a fire at Sitting Log and we have s'mores what got stretchy-marshmallow-sticky all over my chin like a beard. Momma had a good idea to burn up her angry, so I do it too.

I catch the corner on fire and drop it in. My angry goes *whoosh* like hmm … not like a toilet flush, not really like a car start. Oh, I know, like on a airplane when the sound comes from sink drain: Whoosh! But this sound goes away up to the sky instead of just down. I think that God taked it up, the smoke and angry. The paper ashes blow on me, and some stick to my stretchy-marshmallow-sticky chin.

It's gone now, the angry. All gone.

My dad is gone too, to me anyway. He is here for someone, but not me. It might not be permanent. Momma says that forgiveness is for anyone, but we still can't have Dad home. He's not well, she says. I am weller than I think I ever was before because of forgiving. That's what Momma teached me.

I think to fly would be a fun thing right now. I could fly right up, off of Sitting Log, into the sky and see the whole world, and in it, Dad. But that's not real, so I sit with Momma on Sitting Log until the fire goes out dark.

Then my bath time comes, and all the sticky and ashes go glub, glub, glub down the drain. I am clean and feel good.

# PART III

# CHAPTER

*June - July 1, 1989*

---

The mountains are calling, and I must go.
—John Muir

---

Laying out in the sun with Gwen and my sister Erica while the kids splash and swim in the six-foot-diameter, eighteen-inch-deep play pool is a pleasant summer tradition. The June sun sizzles our baby oil slathered skin to a golden brown. We lie on wet towels and run cool hose water over us as we bake. We flip like pancakes when the timer goes off.

It's been seven months since the walk in the forest with Erica and Mom when I decided to add art and horses to our lives, and I have seen a change. Ethan is more self-controlled. His teacher said that, before spring break, she would have recommended repeating kindergarten, but now she believes he will be ready for first grade in the fall. Mrs. Perkins knew I was okay with the possibility of having him retained, but I was glad to hear that she deemed him ready. She gave me a packet of academics to work on over the summer, and we are continuing our riding and art lessons. She says it is amazing to see how much progress children make in just a few months with the right guidance. I think, *It is amazing how fast they digress in a few minutes of trauma.*

"Hey, let's go to the cabin!" I suggest, suddenly inspired. "It's so hot here, and it would be a great getaway. The lodging is free!"

"I like the sound of that!" Gwen says.

"We can go over the Fourth of July for Prescott Frontier Days. I'll put in a request for a couple of days off, and we can stay five days."

"We're in," Gwen says.

"We'll go too," Erica says. "Gwen, you may not bring Stuart."

"Heavens no! I haven't seen him in over a month. I am single and lovin' it. Really, for the first time in my life, I am lovin' it!" Gwen runs the hose water over her head to cool off and grins widely.

The kids play boat with a raft floating in the little pool. They make a whirlpool, all walking clockwise while the child on the raft spins. Then, on the count of three, they turn against the current and squeal as the rapids knock them down. Staying wet helps us tolerate the scorching Palm Desert heat, that and leaving town.

## July 1, 1989

Two weeks later, we head to the cabin. Erica and Paul and their children, Gwen and her children, and Ethan, Roamy, and I meet at the cabin and unload cars. Once we are semiorganized, we venture into town.

People gather in Prescott in the summertime from cities across the Sonoran Desert—; Phoenix, Tucson, and Palm Desert—, to escape the intense heat. Prescott is not exactly cool during the day, but it is about twenty degrees cooler than Palm Desert. If it's 92 degrees in Prescott, it's about 112 degrees at home. The nighttime low temperatures in the mountains are where the real difference is felt.

Prescott Frontier Days draws tens of thousands of people. Food vendors and crafters fill the town square, and a bluegrass band plays patriotic-themed songs in the band shell. The adults munch on kettle corn while our kids share various colors of cotton candy.

Paul and Erica's family stay in Towne Square, while Gwen and I take our kids to the rodeo.

The Oldest Rodeo in the World is celebrating its 101$^{st}$ anniversary. Over one hundred years ago, ranchers and cattlemen had cowboy contests to show townspeople their skills. It's as American as apple pie and a perfect way to spend Independence Day.

Disagreement continues about where the first rodeo actually took place. Pecos, Texas, is bent out of shape over the claim by Prescott. Pecos actually sued Trivial Pursuit over the claim as a game question. The history and realness of the rodeo makes it all the more exciting. Rodeo showcases the abilities of cowboys to do their jobs. The danger is real too. I love baseball and football, but these man-and-beast competitions seem more authentic.

We hold out our arms for wristbands, and Ethan says, "Why?"

"So that they know we belong." I think for a moment that he will throw a fit because of this unexpected requirement, but he holds out his arm and actually smiles. This is new. He usually has to ponder the unexpected, has a meltdown, or gets angry like he did on school picture day.

"We belong, Momma!"

"Yep."

We make our way up the stands and find a bench with enough room for all five of us to sit together. The man next to me is leaning forward with his forearms on his knees and shading his face with a cowboy hat. He watches intently as a cowboy rides a bucking bull in the ring. When the cowboy is thrown to the ground, the rodeo clowns distract the bull while the cowboy makes a speedy exit.

"He got a good long ride," the man next to me says. I smile, and then he looks up and grabs a drink handed to him from the aisle.

"I see you've met Kate and Ethan." The voice from the aisle is familiar.

"Not formally. *The* Kate … and Ethan?" the man in the cowboy hat exclaims.

I turn toward the familiar voice. "Grayson! What? Of course you would be here." I fumble through the initial shock and then try to sort out what the man next to me meant by *the* Kate and Ethan. Is that a good thing or what? I feel like a juvenile and can't speak.

Gwen just sits, stares, and grins, and she doesn't help me out at all.

The man next to me moves over, leaving space for Grayson.

Two girls squeeze past and find their spots on the other side of the men.

Grayson says, "This is my brother, Rylan. Rylan, Kate and Ethan."

Rylan is as handsome as his brother. He has a darker complexion but the same kind smile.

"This is my friend Gwen and her children, Carson and Monique."

"Those two are my girls, Rachel and Annika," Grayson says.

Rylan gently elbows the one next to him, and the girls stop giggling long enough to wave hello.

During all the time that we had been riding with Grayson, we had never met his girls. I asked once if he had a family. Grayson replied that he had two daughters and that his wife had passed away. He didn't say any more than that, and it was none of my business, so I didn't bring it up again.

Annika has the same lean build as her father, the blue eyes and long, wavy, sandy-blonde hair pulled back in an unbrushed ponytail. She's eight years old and sweet as can be.

Rachel is eleven, and her glossy dark brown hair hangs in a sheet to her waist. She's neat as a pin, has piercing green eyes, and is very conscious of the cute boy seated behind her, something I notice even as she chats and giggles with her little sister. Her body language gives her away as she twists her silky tresses over to one side and steals a glance his way.

The afternoon sun is warm, and I hope my pink cheeks and

suntanned complexion help conceal the fact that I am blushing for being so awkward, surprised, and pleased to see Grayson. At the very least, I hope that Grayson and Rylan don't notice. I know Gwen sees right through my nonchalant conversation over the next few minutes, and I cast a glance her way that says, clearly, "Wipe that smirk off your face!"

Then she laughs.

"What did we miss?" Rylan says.

"Nothing." I turn back to Gwen and widen my eyes to give her the universal, "Come on, stop it" sign.

Ethan makes his way over to Grayson and shows him a knot he tied around his leg with a rope he found.

"That's a good quick-release knot, Ethan," Grayson says. Ethan learned it from Grayson tying up the horses.

Annika beckons to Ethan. "Come 'ere. Let me show you one." Ethan parks himself between the girls, and Annika ties him a lasso. "Dad, let me lasso your hand," she says.

Grayson raises his hand, puts pinkie and index fingers up to make a bull, and Annika lassos it, tightening the rope around his wrist with expertise. Ethan is all grins and giggles, and the girls dote on him for the rest of the rodeo show.

When barrel racing starts, Annika pats Ethan on the knee. "Watch this! This is what I am gonna do!" Her eyes are glued to the ring. Ethan follows her gaze and is enthralled with the show of precision and speed.

The afternoon performance passes quickly. We leave with the crowds. Dust clouds billow around us.

"This has been a really great day," I remark to no one in particular.

"Nice," Grayson says with an easy smile.

"We're meeting Kate's sister and her family at the ice cream parlor. We'd love it if y'all would join us," Gwen says.

"Yes, please! We would!" Rachel looks at her dad with those bright green eyes, and it is settled.

We wander along Whiskey Row and run into several neighbors

and high school friends from Palm Desert. It is always like this in Prescott over the Fourth. We meet up with Erica, Paul, and their kids at the ice cream parlor and have dessert before dinner.

"Eat your ice cream now, and if you are still hungry, you can have hamburgers for dessert," I say to the children, teasingly.

"That's a little unorthodox, isn't it?" Ethan says.

"Do you know what that means?" I say. His vocabulary surprises me again.

"Yeah, awkward," he says.

Overhearing, Rylan and Grayson, being brothers who think alike, both reach for Ethan's ice cream cone. Grayson says. "I'll take that cone then. Don't want you feeling uncomfortable about it. Ha-ha."

"No, you won't. You don't like Rocky Road!" Ethan giggles and runs away. He bursts through the group of us, and then he stops as if he's seen a ghost. His mouth drops open. He drops the double scoops off of the cone, and I follow his gaze. Jace stares straight at Ethan. He's not close, but the look on his face tells me that he saw the whole interaction between Ethan and Grayson.

Ethan breaks eye contact to find his cone missing its ice cream. His bottom lip pops out, and his eyebrows press together. He stoops to pick up the dropped ice cream, and Grayson helps him. It's full of dirt, pebbles, and twigs.

"Now that's Rocky Road," Grayson says quietly. "Let's go get you another one."

"That's Rocky Road."

*That's pretty funny*, I think, *and it's sticky.*

"Grayson, it's sticky too cuz ... the sticks."

He laughs at that.

I'm walking back to the ice cream parlor with Grayson, away from my dad. Grayson holds my hand all the way. I am thirsty, so he picks me up high for a drink at the drinking fountain. We get me a double scoop of Rocky Road—but without rocks. He-he.

"Be careful, young man," the scooper guy says. "Your daddy might not buy you a third one."

He's not my daddy. He's my friend. A daddy-sized friend. That's pretty cool. We go back down the street to the park and our families, and I don't see my dad anymore. My ice cream is dripping down my hand, and I make a point on the top of the scoop with my lips. Annika says I have a brown beard and mustache. I lick it off as far as my tongue can reach and wipe the rest on my sleeve.

After ice cream, we run around a lot and play freeze tag. Carson, Annika, Rachel, my cousins Alex and Trevor, and I are all good at the rules. Monique and my twin cousins, Caitlyn and Jack, are not. They won't freeze when we tag them, but we let them play how they want to because they are little.

Too soon, it is time to go back to the cabin for dinner. Uncle Paul grills hamburgers, and we eat them for dessert cuz we had ice cream for dinner. That is *unorthodox*. I had that word from TV. G'ma says it means 'not normal,' but unorthodox is funner to say.

After bath time, Momma tucks me in the bottom bunk in the boys' bunkroom and reads us *The Little Rabbit Who Wanted Red Wings*. Carson thinks it is a story for babies, but I say it's not. The story says to be happy who you are, and I am. Sometimes when I really wish, I wish for a dad like Grayson.

"Momma, the scooper man in the ice cream parlor thought Grayson was my daddy."

"Well, that's an understandable assumption, don't you think?" Momma says.

I nod my head. "Will my dad come to the cabin?"

"Absolutely not."

"Okay. Good night, Momma."

"Good night, Ethan. Good night, boys."

Gwen takes care of the girls. Erica and Paul wash dishes. Then we sit on the deck with a bottle of wine and listen to the crickets and some far-off, early fireworks. Wind whistles softly through the ponderosa pines. I wrap myself in a wool blanket and breathe in the cool mountain air. I love to come here to relax, unwind, and center myself. We look at the stars. I think we all need a little quiet for our souls.

# CHAPTER

*July 2, 1989*

---

Life is the most wonderful fairy tale of all.
—Hans Christian Andersen

---

When I wake up, Gwen already has a cup of coffee and is sitting in her bed in the room we're sharing, reading.

"I put *Star Wars* on the VCR for the kids who are up," she says.

"Who's up?"

"Everyone under the age of twenty-nine," Gwen says with a smile.

"Wow. They're being so quiet."

"Maybe they used up all their words yesterday with Grayson's girls. They sure had fun together. So, what's the deal with Grayson Bennett? You never told me he's a single dad."

"It isn't relevant in terms of what we are doing with the horses, the therapy and all."

"Well, Kate, you might want to rethink what is going on with the horses' owner because I think he's quite taken with you."

"Don't be silly. He is very professional. I will say that he takes a healthy interest in Ethan. Ethan has learned a lot from Grayson besides riding and care of horses: how to solve problems, work through issues, and take a moment to think before impulsively reacting. He's good for him."

"Kate, he's good for you."

"I need some coffee, Gwen. I'll leave you to your book."

Gwen's a hopeless romantic. She falls in love much too quickly, and then her marriages fall apart, the relationships end, and she's left to pick up the pieces of her broken heart again. I am not in any position to criticize her for it, and she knows this about herself.

She says, "When it comes to men, my picker is broke."

I don't even have a *picker*—no time for that—but every so often, it is fun to dream of the perfect fairy-tale life. I smile at her suggestion that Grayson could be interested in me.

"Here comes my sweet boy! Good morning," I say.

Ethan jumps in front of me and waves his "imagilary" light saber at an "imagilary" bad guy.

"Thank you, Ethan Skywalker. Would you like some Cheerios now?"

"Froot Loops."

"Cheerios with twelve Froot Loops on top."

"Okay."

The rest of the children hear the words Froot Loops and scurry to the kitchen for breakfast. Bowls clank, milk spills, and bananas are sliced and distributed to each child's cereal.

Ten minutes later, the kids finish and leave to dress for the day. I wash the dishes, eat the remaining banana, and wash down my toast with cold coffee. Such is my fairy-tale life. Ethan and Roamy run through the kitchen on their way to go play outside.

"Hey, you need to feed her," I say to Ethan.

"Oh, yeah."

When the phone rings, I answer, thinking it'll be Mom calling to check in. It is Grayson. He and Rylan would like to take Gwen and me out dancing at the Saloon tonight. The happy-hour specials are going all weekend long for the holiday, and they have live country music and karaoke on Sunday night. I put my hand over the receiver and call to Gwen.

"Sounds great," she says. "What kind of dancin'?"

"Country swing. I can show you how to do it." I take my hand off of the receiver and say, "That sounds fun, but I'll have to see if Erica and Paul are willing to watch all seven kids tonight."

"Tell you what," Grayson says. "Rachel's a great babysitter, and Annika can help with the little ones if you'd like us to bring them over. Or we can leave them with my folks. It's your call."

"Let me call you back on that. Thank you." We say our goodbyes and hang up.

"What did I tell you?" Gwen says.

"What did you tell her?" Erica says as she and Paul come back from their walk in the woods.

We lay out the plans to Paul and Erica, and it is decided to have Rachel and Annika come help them with the younger children. We confirm with Rylan and Grayson, and they will pick us up and drop off the girls after we feed our kids their dinner.

That afternoon, I put on some music and show Gwen the basics of country swing dancing. Gwen's enthusiastic, and she catches on quickly. When she steps in the wrong direction, she does it with gusto and acts as if that is how it's supposed to be done. Honestly, Gwen's so cute she could probably stand in a box on the dance floor and everyone would think she was belle of the ball. Carson and Ethan cannot stop laughing as they watch us.

"All right, boys. Your turn." I put on the B-52s and crank up the volume to "Rock Lobster." Carson and Ethan dance wildly and call us over.

"Mom, rock out!" Ethan shakes his hair, and Carson mirrors his moves, completely uninhibited. Gwen and I join in, bouncing to the rhythm of the song, and we all sing along.

We were at the beach (Eww)
Everybody had matching towels (Eww)

Somebody went under a dock (Eww)
And there they saw a rock (Eww)
It wasn't a rock (Eww)
Was a rock lobster (Eww) ...
Down, down ...

Monique, Caitlyn, and Jack peer through the spindles on the upstairs railing with bewildered expressions on their faces. The music continues, and we bounce around to the end of the song. Then the little ones join us to dance to "Love Shack." We all crash onto the couch in a heap at the end, laughing and panting from lack of oxygen at our high-altitude dance party. And I look forward to our evening.

# CHAPTER

*July 2, 1989*

---

> You can discover more about a person in an hour of
> play than in a year of conversation.
> —Plato

---

Momma is going out without me, and Carson's mom too. They practice dancing and do their hair all poufed and spray on perfume. They dress in jeans with the shoes what Momma calls city-girl cowboy boots what are not the ones she rides in. Me and Roamy watch them drive out the driveway 'til the red lights on the back of the truck are gone past the trees.

I sit down on the front steps. The chirping is louder here in the forest. The stars cover the whole sky.

Aunt Erica comes out and says, "Listen to the crickets."

"Is that what it is? 'Cause I always thought it was the stars." That's unsettling. *Unsettling* means you always thought one thing—and now you find out it is wrong. Momma told me that word. I wonder ... if more stars are here in the mountains and more chirpings too, how does Aunt Erica know the sound is crickets? She gives me a hug on my shoulder and scruffles my hair. Then we go inside.

Me and Carson are playing Monopoly with the big kids, but Rachel is playing dress-ups with the little kids cuz she's their babysitter. Today we taught Momma and Miss Gwen to rock out really crazy, and that was fun. Momma said they will be "more composed" tonight and do the swing moves like you're supposed to. I guess that is fun when you are old and twenty-something, but I like rock and roll.

Gwen, Grayson, and Rylan chat easily as we drive into town, but I feel my chest tighten. I find it hard to breath. I open the window to let in some fresh air. This is my first date with anyone other than Jace since I was fifteen years old—fourteen years ago. The night air feels good. The anxiety passes, and I join the conversation.

Rylan and Gwen hit it off really well. She is so calm and poised … and southern. She's had some failed relationships, but she's such a wonderful woman. Rylan is an attractive man, thirty-two years old, and has never been married. He lives in his own house on the ranch with Grayson. He helps Grayson with the horses, but he also has what he calls his day job, doing something with computers. Grayson is thirty-four and is the traditional, full-time rancher in the family. They used to have cattle, but now they just have the horses. Teaching riding lessons is a side job Grayson fell into at the request of friends who wanted their kids to learn. He developed his equine-therapy program after seeing some of his more troubled students really benefit from riding and caring for the horses. Through trial and almost no error, he started his fast-growing business. He is presenting his findings to some colleagues in the psych/child development department at California State University, San Bernardino.

His first pursuit is breeding and raising horses, and he's done well with that too. He breaks them, trains them to varying degrees, depending on the buyer, and then he sells them. He boards some of those horses at his ranch.

We park quite a distance from the Saloon, and walk the cobbled sidewalk in the cool evening. Whiskey Row is crowded tonight. Janet and Barry are here with a couple I don't know. We chat with them, and it is nice to catch up on their lives. They just returned from a jaunt to Europe.

A group of guys I know from ASU are here, and I turn away so that they don't see me, but it's a second too late. They are some of the friends Jace kept after our divorce, and I feel squeamish about talking to them. In some cases, the friend of my ex is my friend. This is not one of those cases. They are not mean. It's just awkward. Dan, a sweet, mutual friend who always wants to see Jace and me get back together—more for the nostalgia than the reality that it would ever work—spots me, smiles, and nods.

When we arrive at the Saloon, the place is crowded, loud, and smoky. A large dance floor contains half the crowd. In a barber's chair, a bartender mixes a margarita straight into the open mouth of a girl wearing lots of makeup. Her platinum-blonde curls hang off the sides of the headrest. She waits like a baby bird for the bartender to stop pouring, closes her mouth, shakes her head to mix her drink, swallows, and lets out a loud yelp, then stumbles into the waiting arms of a man with a huge belt buckle.

We get some beers at the bar and move into the crowd to shout our conversation to each other while loud country music weaves around us, pulling us to the dance floor. We make our way to the center and dance to several songs. Grayson is a great dancer, and following his lead, I feel like I did pretty well. Other than our dance session this afternoon, I have not country swing-danced since college.

We break for a fresh beer, and Gwen and Rylan come over to join us.

"Gwen rode the mechanical bull! Ya shoulda seen her!" Rylan beams with enthusiasm.

"It was fun, Kate. You should try it!" Gwen laughs and takes a big swig of her beer. She looks at each of us, pausing almost imperceptibly at each smiling face in her line of sight: first me, then Grayson, then Rylan. Grayson wraps his arm around my waist. It feels very natural, and I slip my arm around him too.

Karaoke has begun, and Gwen and I signed up to sing together. We are committed. We've switched to Cokes and talk over our parts at a table not far from the current performer who is quite funny as he prepares to sing. When he begins singing, we stop talking to watch. His deep voice is perfectly suited for the song.

*This is going to be fun.* I feel like I felt before my theater debut when I played an ear of corn in the second-grade Thanksgiving pageant. I mention that memory to Gwen. She slaps her hand on the table. "Shut up! Really? Oh, we got this!"

We are giddy and nervous. I'm pretty sure Grayson and Rylan don't know what to make of us right now. Our names are announced, and we jump up and quickly make our way to the stage.

"Break a leg!" calls Grayson. He and Rylan settle in their chairs with expressions of calm anticipation.

The emcee is having as much fun as the singers while he announces the songs. "It says here that you will be singing 'These Boots are Made for Walkin'' recorded by Nancy Sinatra in 1966. Let's give a warm welcome to Kate and Gwen!"

We look at each other, grip our mics, and the lyrics scroll up the screen in front of us while the music plays. We alternate lines and sing the refrain together. With each verse, cheers from the audience get louder. I adopt a southern accent, and we ham it up a little more.

You keep saying you got something for me,
Something you call love but confess,
You've been a'messin' where you shouldn't've been a'messin,
And now someone else is getting all your best.
Well, these boots are made for walking, and that's just what they'll do.
One of these days these boots are gonna walk all over you...

We finish with a bow to the audience, and everyone claps. I catch a glimpse of Rylan and Grayson applauding, and I scan the crowd of smiling faces as we make our way back to our seats.

That's when I see Jace glaring at me. I haven't seen him since yesterday when Ethan dropped his ice cream. I didn't know he was here. His face shows a mixture of anger and hurt like I've never seen before, and the lyrics from our song send chills through my body. My face feels frozen as I contemplate what he must be thinking. Gwen and I picked the song because it was short, simple, and had no real high notes that we could mess up. I didn't even think about the lyrics before they rolled up the screen of the karaoke machine. I paid little attention to them as we sang—at least as they pertained to me or us ... Jace and me, that is.

"I gotta go. I'll be right back." I squeeze Grayson's hand for reassurance.

Gwen looks puzzled and turns to see where I am heading. Full comprehension hits her when she sees Jace. "Do you want me to go with you?"

"No, thanks. I'll be right back." I walk toward Jace, thinking I'll just say that I am sorry if he thought our song was in any way directed at him, because it was not. Not at all.

When I approach him, he is livid—and drunk. "You really outdid yourself this time, Kate! You just had to rub salt in the wound! First your friend moves in on my kid, and then you throw it in my face with your stupid song!"

"Jace, I am sorry if—"

"Get lost." He turns away, downs another shot of tequila, grabs his beer bottle, and walks out the door.

When I turn around, Grayson, Rylan, and Gwen are right behind me. I tear up a bit, partly because I am humiliated and partly because a little piece of me still wants acceptance from Jace.

Grayson wraps me up in a big bear hug. "Move on, Kate." He kisses me on the forehead. The crowd and the noise, which were so much fun just moments ago, close in on me.

Gwen bites her lip and looks for a quiet place to sit. "Let's go for a walk. We can come back in a little while."

"We'll all go," Rylan says.

Quaint streetlamps light the cobblestone sidewalk. It's as crowded with people as it was earlier and a lot rowdier. A man on a unicycle is juggling in a parking lot, and a small crowd has gathered to watch. We join them, and my friends seem to have put aside the incident with Jace. A pair of street musicians play dueling banjos while people drop change into their open banjo cases. Crowds of people and bumper-to-bumper traffic in the street offset the small-town feel. Teens squeal their tires when the traffic light changes to green. They hang from truck windows and shout to friends. Why couldn't they shout a warning? Did anyone see the enraged man with the broken beer bottle running up behind us? But no one is paying attention to us. It happens in a flash. We are watching the juggler on the unicycle, dueling banjo music adding to the energy in the air, and I see a flash in the corner of my eye.

# CHAPTER 37

*July 2, 1989*

---

> Provide for those who grieve in Zion to bestow on
> them a crown of beauty instead of ashes, the oil of joy
> instead of mourning, and a garment of praise instead
> of a spirit of despair.
> —Isaiah 61:3 (NIV)

---

Jagged broken glass where the base of the bottle used to be whirls past me and catches Grayson in the lower back. Jace lunges again and slashes Grayson deeply in the arm. Blood gushes from his brachial artery. Grayson turns and pushes Jace away hard and readies himself to fight. Rylan kicks the bottle from Jace's hand, and it shatters on the cobblestone. The two brothers wrestle Jace to the ground. All eyes turn from the unicyclist to us.

I hear the sound of my own voice as if it is coming from someplace else. "Somebody help!" I look for a pay phone, but I don't see one.

As Grayson continues to bleed heavily, the color drains from his face. He teeters, loses his grip on Jace, and falls to the ground. Gwen and I rush to apply pressure to his wounds.

Jace looks stunned when Rylan releases his grip. Spit sprays Jace in the face as Rylan curses him and shoves him to the sidewalk again. Then he rushes to relieve Gwen at Grayson's back.

Concerned people from the crowd form a ring of protection and curiosity around us. A bystander gives his name and number to Gwen as a witness. A police officer pushes through the crowd and radios for an ambulance. Witnesses hurriedly tell him what happened and point to Jace.

Jace gets up from the sidewalk where Rylan left him. He staggers, pauses, and looks over his shoulder. He winces as if the entirety of his life's pain strikes him in the gut. "Katie, I didn't mean for this to happen. Really. It's not your fault. It's mine."

He steps into the street and walks out from between the parked cars just as the traffic light changes and the tires squeal. The thud is sickening. I am already agonizing over Grayson, my face wet with tears. The horror of what I think may have just happened to Jace strikes a blow to my chest, and cold rushes through my body. My hands are sopped with blood. I press with all of my strength, and the blood keeps flowing. Grayson moans, and horrified onlookers switch their focus from us to the street, where lies the crumpled body that was my husband. The boy I loved in high school. The one with so much potential who chose poorly, and now, is presumably gone.

He was angry with me tonight. I forgave him for everything in our past the night Ethan and I burned our paintings in the campfire. Not knowing that, Jace thought our karaoke song was directed at him. What was it he said to me as he walked away? He looked remorseful. Dismal. He said something like, "Katie, I didn't mean for this to happen … it was my fault."

What did he mean? Was he sorry for being an abusive husband and a terrible father and ending up divorced? Getting angry about the song, lashing out and stabbing Grayson? Did he walk into the street on purpose? At the first court-ordered visit with Ethan, he looked defeated when he left. Had he completely lost hope for a better future?

No one can know the thoughts he had in those last moments.

Maybe it was regret he dwelt on right then. And now, is he really gone? My heart is heavy as I wrap my mind around what is happening. My hands press the artery, but it's slippery. I need to adjust my grip.

"Please stay with me, Grayson!"

I feel a hand on my shoulder and am relieved to see that help is here. EMTs are taking over. Gwen, Rylan, and I are covered with blood, and an EMT asks if we are injured. Gwen's chin trembles as she tells an EMT what happened. I'm in a fog.

They have no room in the ambulance for Rylan, so he will have to drive himself to the hospital. The sound of sirens gets louder as more police and emergency vehicles arrive. Police disperse the crowd. The people back up, but they don't leave. They watch, as if it's a show, but no one smiles or claps now.

An ambulance takes Jace. Maybe he is still alive. The boys from the truck that hit him chatter as police officers take names. The driver is not very old. He says, "He came outta nowhere, stepped right in front of me! I couldn't stop. Oh God. Is he dead? Is he?"

Police officers take notes and talk on radios. Lights from emergency vehicles flash blue and red across the growing crowd of onlookers.

All I hear now is a loud buzz in my head that drowns out the voices, the questions, and the sirens. Everything becomes bright white. I don't feel a thing when I hit the ground.

The next thing I am aware of is a soft surface beneath me, a bumpy ride. A siren blares. I hear voices around me, but they are not talking to me. Someone says, "Her husband is dead." I wonder who they are talking about. *Who is she? Who is her husband? What are they saying?*

"Grayson's not ..."

I hear a woman's voice. "Hey, you're back. Good. What's that you said, Kate?"

"I'm holding on so he doesn't bleed out. I'm not hurt. It's Grayson's blood."

"That's right, sweetie. You did good. He's already on his way to the hospital. But you smacked your head pretty hard when you passed out. We're just going to get you checked out and stitched up."

"Where are we going?"

"To the ER."

"Gwen?"

"Your friend? She's coming with Grayson's brother. She's okay. Shook up, but okay."

I fade out again and sleep the rest of the way to the hospital.

The ambulance stops, the back doors swing open, and I feel the stretcher pulled into the fresh mountain air. The wheels are clicked into place, and I am rolled inside through brightly lit corridors with multiple sets of swinging doors. In a small curtained room, I close my eyes to block the painfully bright light. I gain focus of thought. I appreciate the efficiency of the team that takes over as the EMTs leave.

The woman who rode with me in the ambulance says, "Take care, sweetie." She parts the curtains and walks away.

I picture Jace in the street, and panic clutches at my chest. I try to sit up to catch my breath.

"Stay still, Kate." A man in green scrubs has a syringe in his gloved hand. "I'm going to give you something to help you relax."

"What happened to Jace?"

"You know him?"

"We used to be married." Clarity has returned and, with it, horror.

"I think they are working on him now," he says. "Ready?" Without waiting for an answer, he injects something through my IV. I fall asleep.

When I wake up, Gwen is semi-reclined in a cushioned vinyl chair. "Hey. How are you?"

"My head hurts."

"Have a little water."

I take a sip. The concern on her face frightens me. "What has happened? Where is Grayson? What happened to Jace? Are they okay?"

"Kate, they think Grayson is going to be fine. He lost a lot of blood, and they want to keep him a couple of days for observation. They are still stitching him up." She pauses, takes the water cup from my hand, and puts her hand on my arm. "Kate, Jace didn't make it. He was DOA. They said he died instantly."

My mind whirls. I used to hope he would not make it home to beat me again, but I am not relieved. I feel awful. I remember a conversation we had one time, after our divorce. "Jace, why do you hate me? What have I done?"

He replied, "I don't hate you. I just get so angry. If you were to die, I would come to your funeral—and I would be sad."

It wasn't the profession of enduring love that I wanted, but it was all he had to give. And oddly, it comforted me to hear those words from my ex-husband. I will be sad at his funeral too.

Erica parts the curtains and enters my little space in the emergency room. She looks frantic. When I see my sister's face, I lose all composure. Since I regained consciousness I have been frozen with fear and grief. My younger sister's concerned expression makes me sob.

Erica holds me tight for a long time.

I cry out my grief, my anger, and my fear. God, oh God! If you are real, show me. Why is the answer to my prayers so often, "No?" Layered beneath the immediate trauma, emotions from years ago surge through me. They are released in tears that feel as if they are caught up by love—my sister's and Gwen's—but more. Much more.

I am spent, and my tears are all poured out. The powerful love and strength that I feel lifts my soul in way that is hard to explain. It cannot be contained, but it is in me. The news of Jace's death crushes any hope that his life might improve. A half hour earlier, I thought

I couldn't go on. I was paralyzed, tortured by long-standing grief. Now someone else holds that burden.

I realize now that forgiveness was just the starting point. I took a step forward into a new life by the campfire in our gulley. Smoke swirled, and a breeze gently carried my anger away. A heavy burden was lifted that night, but my sadness remained. I still felt hurt, and I tried to manage that pain on my own.

The permanence of this loss drives me into the arms of God, and he delivers on his promise to be with me always. For a split second, I think that I should feel guilty for receiving emotional healing at a time such as this. However, the love I feel overcomes the guilt and the thought that I don't deserve it. Maybe none of us deserve this love, but it is freely given when we let go. For my whole life I've heard about this God who rebuilds us from ashes and mourning, but I never experienced His love in this way before.

The ash from our burnt watercolor paintings blew away from our campfire into the desert. I have received a beautiful replacement: love, peace, and hope for a new and full life. It feels as if it happened quickly, but as I ponder the path that led me to where I am today, I see that the steps toward this moment have been walked out over many years.

Mrs. Leoni told me that happiness is a choice. After I wallowed in self-pity in the back room for a while, I took her words to heart and practiced embracing a positive outlook. I entered the sales floor that day with new eyes. The consequences of my bad choices no longer overshadow my fortunate life. They are just obstacles that I have overcome.

However, this is a big hurdle. Grayson will heal, but our barely budding relationship might not withstand this. Ethan will no longer be able to hope that his dad will change his ways and become the dad he desires.

Dharma and Natasha Stepanovych are living proof of joy that overcomes sadness in their lives. It's a joy that transcends our capacity to make it happen on our own. We can't will it into existence, but we can be open to accepting it.

I love Grayson's calm demeanor. He exudes peace with his easy smile, quiet manner, and loving nature. I found out he had a good marriage and the loss of his wife was devastating to him and his girls. He is strong, physically and in character, but I think the thing that carries him through that pain is his strong faith. I hope he is okay. I pray for him and for his girls. I pray for Ethan. This time, I know my prayers are heard.

It is quiet in my little curtained room. The lights have been dim since I woke up, but I stay still and keep my eyes closed. Gwen and Erica's silence shows me that they know I need the quiet to process all that has happened.

A woman with a clipboard appears. Her lipstick is worn off except for an outline around her lips, and strands of hair hang loose from her ponytail at the end of her long shift. It is six o'clock in the morning, and she asks me if I can sit up and sign release papers.

My head pounds, and I see stars when I sit abruptly in my bed.

"Slowly!" she says. "Let's just raise the head of the mattress." She pushes the button to raise my head, bit by bit, until I am upright enough to sign papers. She hands me a little plastic cup of cran-apple juice and encourages me to drink it all. "X-rays show no sign of fracture," she says. "Don't wash your hair for three days. You want to keep the stitches dry and covered. You have a concussion, so no contact sports, no TV, and no fireworks until a doctor clears you."

The way my head feels now, I don't want to hear a door close, much less fireworks.

"All of your instructions are here," she says to me, and shows them to Erica and Gwen. "Take your time getting up."

The clean clothes Erica brought me smell Downy fresh in contrast to the antiseptic aroma all around us. Gwen grabs the large plastic bag that contains my personal belongings. I notice for the first time that Gwen is wearing a clean sweater that covers the blood-spattered outfit from last night.

She sees me looking, buttons the cardigan, and says, "Last night, a lady on the street gave this to me. Erica brought me clean clothes. I'll change when we get you out of here."

The lady with the clipboard reappears with a wheelchair, but I prefer to walk. Erica holds my arm, and I shuffle to the waiting room where Rylan drinks a large cup of coffee.

He points to a cardboard caddy containing three more coffees, three water bottles, and a bag of bagels. "Grayson's out of the woods. He's resting right now. They moved him to a room where they can observe him and make sure the sutures don't rupture and that he has no internal bleeding. We can go up when you are ready."

The coffee warms me, and the bagels fill the void in my stomach. My balance has improved, but the bright light stabs my eyes like darts. I take a moment to rest. Gwen takes the opportunity to go change her clothes.

I see that Rylan has blood on his clothes too. I imagine the puddle on the cobblestone sidewalk and gulp back the tight feeling in my throat. I turn away from them and wipe my eyes with my sleeve. "I'm ready."

Gwen is back in clean clothes, and we step into the elevator.

# CHAPTER 38

*July 3, 1989*

---

Into each life some rain must fall. Some days must be
dark and dreary.
—Henry Wadsworth Longfellow

---

Grayson is nested on billowy pillows, and he groggily looks our way when we arrive. There is an IV in his arm. I hope that whatever is dripping into his vein keeps him comfortable. The rhythmic beeping of his monitor keeps the nurses at their station down the hall.

From across the bed, a man in his fifties, tall and lean, looks at me with familiar pale blue eyes.

"I'm so sorry," I say. He gives me a nod. Rylan introduces him as his father, John Bennett, and we shake hands. He slumps in his chair, scanning his son, the gauze bandages, the tubes and wires. He rests his head back and closes his eyes.

Rylan introduces his mother, Dotty. To my surprise, she gives me a hug. "How are you holding up, dear? Do you need a chair? I hear that you have had quite a night!"

"I'm okay. No, you sit. I've been prone for hours. It feels good to stretch my legs."

Gwen told me earlier that they were stitching Grayson up. That was an understatement. The vascular surgeon says that the bottle cut Grayson like a dozen knives, and the brachial artery was severed almost all the way through. Apparently, because of the pseudo-medical training I had with Dad and some amazing supernatural guidance, I saved Grayson's life during those first few minutes before the EMTs arrived. I just did what made sense in the moment. Fortunately, he suffered no peripheral nerve damage.

I look around for the girls, and Dotty reads my mind. "Children under twelve cannot visit. They are at your place with Paul. They have been kept up to date and have strict instructions to say nothing to the other children until you have a chance to talk to Ethan."

"Thank you," I say.

After a brief visit Rylan, Gwen, Erica, and I leave to go home to the cabin. I ride with Erica and ponder how to talk to Ethan. I absorb the scenery as we drive past old Victorian houses on quaint residential streets and then pine trees as we leave Prescott behind and drive up the steep dirt road to the cabin. When we park, I take in the view of the valley as we discuss the best way to tell Ethan that his dad is dead.

Uncle Paul says my momma bonked her head and had to get stitches. I had those before. I want to play with Annika, but she isn't in the mood. Aunt Erica left to get Momma before I got up this morning. I've just been waiting with Carson and Roamy. We made a tent in our bunk beds and played camping with flashlights. I wrote my name under the top bunk with a blue crayon so everyone will always know I was there. Uncle Paul made us happy-face pancakes with whipped cream just like at IHOP.

Momma's here now, and she gives me a hug. "Carson, your mom will be here soon. Girls, Uncle Rylan is on his way for you. Ethan, let's go to my room."

"I want to show you my tent," I say.

Momma nods, and we go upstairs to our bunk room.

"Ethan, that is a great tent. It's like you have a whole campsite with your flashlights and all."

Momma says she wants to lie down. I hold the hang-down blanket back so we can lie on my bunk.

She hugs me and looks at me hard. Roamy snuggles in with us. "Ethan, I was not the only person who got hurt last night. Grayson is going to be okay, but he did get hurt. He has to stay in the hospital for a few days."

I look up at my name under the top bunk. Momma sees it too. She is not mad even though I wrote on fruniture.

"I have something to tell you, Ethan." She stops talking for a second or a minute. "Your dad was in town last night. He had an accident, and he died."

I feel a shock go through my body like lightning.

"He's dead?"

"Yes."

"Permanent forever?"

"Yes."

I shine my flashlight on my name. "I will still guard you."

"Okay, Ethan. Thank you."

"Can I go play with Carson now?"

"Yes."

I go downstairs with Roamy. Momma stays in my tent.

# CHAPTER

*July 4, 1989*

---

With the past, I have nothing to do; nor with the
future. I live now.
—Ralph Waldo Emerson

---

Independence Day begins with an explosive headache. Throbbing pain beats me with the reality that my nightmare is real. My eyes clamp shut against the sun, and I wish for a time machine to take me back, just two days, where the facts of what has transpired will not haunt me.

Roamy has her front paws on the edge of the bed. I feel her moist breath on my face.

"Hi, Roamy."

She wags her whole body in appreciation of the acknowledgement, and then she bounds downstairs.

My head pounds as I make my way to the bathroom. I pause to scrutinize my reflection. My pajamas are really old, and I look older too. My hair's a mess. I can't wash it, but Gwen managed to clean it one strand at a time with a washcloth to get the blood out. For that, I am grateful.

I stretch my neck and pop some Tylenol. I feel like I am looking at someone else through a window. She's a little older than I am and appears to have had a hard life. The dark circles under her eyes make her look exhausted and ill. She looks back at me like she is asking for answers. "Sorry, girl. I have no answers."

I splash cold water onto my ashen skin, and some color comes to my cheeks. I brush my teeth and hair, careful to avoid the stitches in my head, and put on a sundress and some Vaseline on my lips. Then I head downstairs.

"Good morning, sunshine," Erica says. "Have some French toast."

The kids laugh and run around outside. Roamy bounces through the tall grass and wild flowers as if it was a normal day.

Erica says, "Gwen said she and the Bennetts are going into town and can take any of the kids who want to go to fireworks tonight. Paul and I will stay here with you and watch fireworks from the deck. We should be able to see them, and it won't be loud at all."

"Thanks, Erica. That's sweet of you. You don't mind staying here?"

"Nope. It'll be a nice quiet evening."

I gobble up the French toast and then walk outside, squinting with a hand shading my eyes. The boys erected a fort under a huge ponderosa pine, and I duck inside. Hunched in their den, I smooth pine needles and take a seat.

"Ethan, do you want to go to fireworks tonight?"

"Are you going?"

"No. I have to stay here, but I'll see them in the distance from our deck."

"I'll do that."

"Stay here?"

"Yes. I don't like the loud."

"Okay. I'm going to see Grayson this afternoon. Will you be okay here with Carson and Uncle Paul?"

"No."

"No?"

"You might not come back. You might get hurt and never see me again."

"Hmm. Well, that's not likely, but I'll stay here with you for today."

"For forever."

"I don't think you will want that when you go to first grade."

"I will."

"Okay. Give me a hug. I'm going inside."

Once inside, I ask, "Erica, can you keep an eye on Ethan? I'm going to call Grayson. I'm not going to see him today."

"Sure, take your time."

"Thanks."

The phone rings long enough for Grayson to reach it. When he doesn't answer, I hang up and call the nurses' station. A soft-spoken nurse assures me that he is just sleeping. With the information that he is okay and the warmth of the sun heating my room, I fall asleep. After my nap, my head feels quite a bit better.

Voices become clearer as I tread downstairs. The Bennetts and Gwen leave for town with a slew of children in two vehicles.

We sit on the deck and wait for the fireworks. Ethan and the twins, Caitlyn and Jack, place peanuts on the railing, and the blue jays gather them up and fly off as the sun sets. The first distant boom places Ethan on my lap.

"Let's count the seconds between the light and the boom, Ethan. It will be like lightning and thunder. Remember, light is fast, and sound is a little slow."

"Look!" Ethan counted. "One, two, three, four, five, six, seven, eight."

Boom!

"Eight. That's pretty far away."

"Do you think Dad can see them?"

"I don't know."

Paul tunes in to a radio station playing patriotic music. The fireworks display is beautiful. The finale is long enough that lights and booms intermingle. Finally, in darkness, we hear the last of the booms followed by crackles as they echo across the valley. Then quiet.

Ethan breaks the silence. "What is next?"

"Bedtime."

"No. I mean for Dad."

"A church service called a funeral where his family and friends can come to say things about him and say goodbye to him. People will pray. Grandma and Grandpa Evans will be there. Then he will be buried. Do you think you want to go?"

"Will you?"

"Yes. I will go."

"Can I sit with you and Grandma and Grandpa Evans?"

"They would love to sit with you, Ethan. I'm not sure about me, so we will see."

"When a person dies, do they go right to heaven—or does it take a long time to get there? Is it fast like light or slow like sound?"

"I guess that it's quick. People die, but they are alive immediately in heaven. To us on earth, Dad is dead, but to God, he is alive. We will see him alive in heaven. Does that make sense?"

"So, fast like light."

"Yes, fast like light." That's a comforting thought. Like the explosion of a firework, the violence lasts a moment and the beauty follows immediately. I feel that same overwhelming love I felt in the hospital. I tighten my arms around my boy and exhale deeply. I think of a verse that I memorized in Sunday school ages ago:

> I pray that you, being rooted and established in love, may have power, together with all the Lord's holy people, to grasp how wide and long and high and deep is the love of Christ, and to know this love that surpasses knowledge—that you may be filled to the measure of all the fullness of God. (Ephesians 3:17b–19, NIV)

# CHAPTER

*July 11, 1989*

---

Life isn't about finding yourself. Life is about creating yourself.
—George Bernard Shaw

---

I mirror Dharma's contagious smile as she passes out incomplete projects from our last art class. We sketched light pencil drawings and then added watercolor. Now we add a layer of color with markers and colored pencils, giving more detail to our paintings. Edges are added to vague shapes, creating buildings. Add highlights of white to a wash of blue water to give it dimension or motion. The details in Ethan's, being the artwork of an almost six-year-old, surprise me. Lines swirl like a wrought iron gate, over a background of sunset-colored paints.

"It's heaven, Momma." He adds some orange circles and ovals. "Look, halos for the ones who are just going there." He wears a vibrant expression as he looks at his heaven.

As I work on the piece in front of me, watery images gain clarity.

"Isn't it amazing how the painting changes with such small additions?" It's the same woman who noticed my "rough-day" painting. Her name is Christine, and her daughter is Leah. We know them pretty well after all these months. We talk frequently at class and have gone for ice cream a couple times with the kids.

"It is." A tiny line can change the mood of a face, give flight to a bird, or add an entry to a building. One incident in life can change everything in much the same way, but we have the ability to choose how the incident affects us. We can create ourselves as defeated or triumphant, resentful or grateful, gloomy or joyful. If we say to ourselves, "I just hold grudges. That's just who I am," then we are giving in to a negativity that grows into resentment and bitterness. It's self-defeating. I know that my willingness to forgive Jace set me free and allowed for more growth in my life. I can see how it helps Ethan too.

Dharma stops to admire each of her student's artwork and encourages each one with legitimate praise. Encouragement flows naturally from her. That is a habit I aim to develop.

She comes to our table. "Kate, that is very good! Your piece has a freedom that I haven't seen from you before. It's delightful! And, Ethan, I love this depiction of heaven. Can you tell me why you chose to paint it this way?"

"It has a gate like in *The Littlest Angel,* and that keeps it safe. And the halos are for the people who go there so they can fly, and so everyone knows they belong, like wristbands do."

"Well, I think that's just grand! Heaven is safe and beautiful," she says.

"If it's safe, I don't know if my dad is allowed in."

His comment surprises me. We talked about this at length. I told Ethan what his dad said to me right before he died: "Katie, I didn't mean for this to happen. Really. It's not your fault. It's mine." I suppose I could be reading too much into it, but I know that God is just and will accept our repentance any time we give it. I have to believe Jace gave it.

"That's a hard thing to think about, isn't it?" Dharma says. "I suppose we won't know what heaven is really like until we get there.

I know that God loves your daddy, and I know he gave him every chance to accept Him. I think that you will find him there when it's your time to go—, in one hundred years."

Ethan smiles and draws a halo leaning against the gate.

# CHAPTER

### July 12, 1989

---

> I may not have gone where I intended to go, but I
> think I have ended up where I needed to be.
> —Douglas Adams, *The Long Dark Tea-Time of the Soul*

---

"G'ma, can you put these ones in water so they stay good? I wanna put them with my dad." I picked them with G'pa while Momma and G'ma have a talk with coffee.

G'ma wraps them in wax paper, ties them with string, puts them in a cup of water, and puts the flowers in a cooler with ice so that they won't wilt. Today is the day what momma told me. The day they put my dad down in the ground. But he's not there, Momma says. The real him already went to heaven, fast like light. Just his body will go to the ground. But I still want to put flowers, in case he visits his body, so he will know I bringed a present for him.

Momma says that his "not well" is well now. That's how heaven works.

I have to wear a not-soft shirt. I don't like that, and since Dad won't be there, I don't know why.

"Ethan, it's time to go home and get dressed now," Momma says.

My cooler is little and red. In it are my flowers, and I put them in the car.

The service for Jace is to take place in an hour. I change into a dark, sleeveless dress, touch up my makeup, and put my hair up in a banana clip. Ethan is dressed and ready to go in his tan shorts and kelly green shirt emblazoned with all four Teenage Mutant Ninja Turtles. I find a plaid short-sleeved button-down to put over the T-shirt.

"Ow! I hate this! It's scratchy!"

I hurriedly cut out the tag. He wears it open, and we are on our way.

Grandma and Grandpa Evans wait for Ethan in front of Chapel on the Desert. The church is old by California standards, built in 1923. Its eighteenth-century Spanish-style architecture makes it feel much older. Ethan holds my hand with both of his hands, which Grandpa notices, and he invites me to sit up front with them.

The organ plays a somber tune as we enter the church. Dim lighting, statues of saints, Mary, and Jesus, and the stunning stained-glass windows are reminiscent of a European cathedral. This chapel is a familiar place—lovely, homey, and comforting rather than cavernous and grand. Friends have been married in this church.

The casket is closed, and Ethan asks Grandpa if he can open it.

"No. Let's look at some pictures to remember him." They walk hand in hand to look at large photos on easels. Ethan studies a photo of Jace as a child.

Grandpa Evans points out a young image of Grandma in the background of the photo and chats with him about Jace. Then he says, "Ethan, I want to know you better. I want to do things with you more often and help you grow up." He dries his eyes with a handkerchief, and Ethan stares at another photo of his dad.

When they come back to our pew, Grandpa Evans puts his hand

on my shoulder. "I want a second chance. I want to make things right." I nod, and he takes a seat next to his wife, who won't even look at me.

The service is short but meaningful. People approach to offer condolences to Jace's parents and include Ethan and me. I am relieved when Suzanne, Mike, and Dylan come over to talk.

Dylan gives Ethan a bag of gummy bears. Mike pats him on the shoulder and says, "Anything you need, Ethan, you let us know."

"Suzanne, thanks for coming." I look over my shoulder and see that Jace's parents have moved quite a distance away, and I whisper, "This is a little awkward."

Gwen and her children approach and join us.

"Has Jace's mom spoken to you yet?" Suzanne says.

"Not a word. But his dad has been kind. You know he's been sober for years now, and he wants to be around for Ethan. Grandma has always been there for Ethan. She's just not fond of me."

"Kate, don't think for a minute that you are to blame for any of the mess Jace made of his life. She may need someone to blame, but not you," Gwen says.

"I don't know if she blames me. I still wonder if I could have done anything—"

"Stop wondering! You did all that you could, dawlin', more than most." Gwen sure has confidence in me.

"She's so crushed. I can't imagine what it would be like to lose your child, even one who's messed up, maybe especially then. And Molly. So awful. I feel bad for them."

"Yeah, well, you have enough on your plate, cleaning up the wreckage Jace imposed on Ethan, and on you," Gwen says.

"Shush. His mom is coming this way," Suzanne says. "We are very sorry for your loss, Mrs. Evans."

She passes without uttering a word, and my heart breaks for her all the more.

Mike and the children are sharing gummy bears when we turn back to them.

"Ethan, we're leaving for the cemetery in two minutes," I say.

Gwen, Suzanne, and Mike promise to get together soon, and we head out.

Our car is sizzling hot. I layer my pocket and skirt of my dress, as a potholder, to grab the metal door handles. I leave the doors open and turn on the air-conditioning. We spread towels on hot vinyl seats and fold the window shade. The ice bottles we brought have melted, and we drink our fill of tepid water.

With headlights on the procession travels unobstructed to the graveyard. We enter through a large wrought iron gate with a white stucco arch and a wall that steps down to about three feet high. Inside the wall, the cemetery is quite simple. Paloverde trees provide a little filtered shade for coveys of quail and some lizards. Crushed granite pathways lead visitors through graves in neat rows. Under a white canopy, white folding chairs mimic the rows of headstones. Astroturf that smells like hot tires surrounds the hole where Jace will be laid to rest.

Ethan walks to the hole's edge and peers to the bottom. He looks at me as if he is about to ask a question, but seeing people who take their seats behind me, he decides to remain quiet. His fistful of flowers from G'ma's garden consists of purple vincas, tiny, white onion blossoms, and leafy gardenia stems. He sits next to me and studies his bouquet. Ethan examines a tiny black bug on one of the flowers, shakes him gently to the ground, and then walks to the casket to lay his flowers on top of it. He hasn't cried about losing his father. He's been stoic all week. He sits next to me, looking glum, and I pat his leg.

The voice of the priest sounds like wind in my ears. I don't discern his words at all. I am thinking of Jace: who he once was, who he became, and now, the child he has left behind. Ethan's lower lip is sticking out, and his eyebrows are pressed together.

This is just the beginning. The threat of harm coming from Jace is over, but unpacking the emotions that Ethan has to face is still ahead of us. We stand for a closing prayer, and then people quietly leave.

Grandma and Grandpa Evans stand at the edge of the grave. Grandma cries, and Grandpa holds her, looking somber.

We say goodbye, and Ethan's grandparents give him hugs. I feel ready to face our future as we head toward the car.

Grayson stands in the shade of a paloverde tree. Beyond the rows of headstones, Rylan waits in his truck. Ethan and I approach Grayson, and he wraps us both up in his one good arm. Grayson and I each take one of Ethan's hands and walk away from Jace for the last time.

# ADDENDUM

There is no love like first love, the strength of it, and the innocence in youth when feelings are new and the belief is that it will last forever. It does, in a way, last forever. Looking back at a first love conjures up nostalgia nothing else holds. If that relationship ends, the loss lingers. The thought remains in the background that if only we could hold onto those feelings towards each other, life could be heaven on earth. However, life is messy and we move on, sometimes trudging through muck that grips us, trying to take us down. Our circumstances can force us to let go of the thing, or the person we love most, knowing that there will never be a first love again.

I think it was that way for both of us. But I guess I will never truly know how the split affected him. I do know that there is power in forgiveness, especially God's forgiveness, and that when we accept forgiveness, the gratitude for that changes us from the inside out. There is healing that comes from forgiving others, even if they never know or acknowledge it. We can recapture a bit of the first love, our side of it anyway, when reconciliation is no longer an option. We can learn to love ourselves again and no longer carry the heavy burden of the pain and anger of the past.

Thirty-four years after the ending of Burning Watercolors takes place we have at our disposal many more options for therapies to help manage mental health and healing from trauma. There is more understanding of brain development. Equine therapy and art therapy have been tested and proven beneficial. Biofeedback, brain training and medications have come a long way in recent decades.

As a volunteer at Royal Family KIDS Camp - a camp for abused children in the foster care system – I've seen how caring interaction during a few days of normalcy and fun can truly change kids' lives. When they choose to believe that God is for them, and people come along who affirm their value, these wounded children can live abundant lives.

Research has shown that it takes five positive experiences to outweigh one negative experience. Children in foster care have experienced the worst kinds of trauma and abuse in their early lives. With approximately twenty thousand moments in a day, we have the opportunity to make those moments positive. A moment is defined as a few seconds in which our brain records an experience. When we make moments matter for these children and create literally hundreds or thousands of positive moments in their days, their brains begin to create new synapses. In just five days at Royal Family KIDS Camp they begin to see themselves in a new light. The follow-up mentor program reinforces that growth. There is hope for these most vulnerable members of our community.

# ACKNOWLEDGEMENTS

I have a lot of gratitude for the friends and family members who encouraged me to write this story. Thank you for the time you took to read and brainstorm with me.

Working with my kindergarten team for seven years was a joy. The experience confirms that Ethan's behavior and language are age appropriate. Every day was an opportunity to bring my best to serve, teach and direct the children in our classroom, and to participate in facilitating their growth as students and as future productive adults.

# NOTES

1. Eric Carl, *The Very Hungry Caterpillar* (Putnam/Philomel (US) 1969)
2. Anna Sewell, *Black Beauty* (Simon and Schuster 1877)
3. Audrey Wood and Don Wood, *King Bidgood's in the Bathtub* (Houghton Mifflin Harcourt 1985)
4. "Jokes: Big List of Clean School Jokes," Ducksters Education Site, accessed June 18, 2017, www.ducksters.com/jokes/school.php
5. "Dharma, Life stages and social stratification" Wikipedia, accessed June 18, 2017, https://en.wikipedia.org/wiki/Dharma
6. Peter Applebome, "Wrangling over Where Rodeo Began," NYTimes.com, June 18, 1989, accessed June 18, 2017, http://www.nytimes.com/1989/06/18/travel/wrangling-over-where-rodeo-began.html?pagewanted=all
7. Carolyn Sherwin Bailey, *The Little Rabbit Who Wanted Red Wings* (New York: Platt and Monk, 1961)
8. Charles Tazewell, *The Littlest Angel* (Ideals Publishing, 1962)

## Lyrics

1. "At Seventeen" by Janis Ian
2. "Rock Lobster," by the B-52s
3. "These Boots are Made for Walkin'" by Lee Hazlewood, recorded by Nancy Sinatra, release date February 22, 1966

# Epigraphs

1. James Baldwin, *Nobody Knows My Name,* (New York: The Dial Press, 1961)
2. Norman Cousins, Goodreads, accessed June 19, 2017, https://www.goodreads.com/quotes/41499-death-is-not-the-greatest-loss-in-life-the- greatest
3. Sigmund Freud quoted by Dorothea Kay Stone, "The Forgotten Parent: The father's contribution to infant development," Auckland Therapy, Counseling and Psychotherapy, 2008, accessed June 19, 2017, http://aucklandtherapy.co.nz/Articles/FathersContribution.htm
4. Graham Greene, *The Power and the Glory,* (Penguin Group (USA) Inc., 1946)
5. Georgia O'Keeffe, BrainyQuote, accessed June 19, 2017, https://www.brainyquote.com/quotes/quotes/g/georgiaok134583.html
6. Aristotle quoted by Philosiblog, "Good habits formed at youth make all the difference." Philosiblog: Home of the Examined Life, April 25, 2011, accessed on June 19, 2017, http://philosiblog.com/2011/04/25/make-all-the-difference/
7. Albert Einstein, Goodreads, accessed June 19, 2017, https://www.goodreads.com/quotes/29875-the-world-is-a-dangerous-place-to-live-not- because
8. Lundy Bancroft, *Why Does He Do That? Inside the Minds of Angry and Controlling Men*, (New York: Penguin Publishing Group, 2003)
9. Ralph Waldo Emerson, Goodreads, accessed June 19, 2017, https://www.goodreads.com/quotes/353-for-every-minute-you-are-angry-you-lose-sixty-seconds
10. Sonya Parker, Author Sonya Parker Quotes, accessed June 19, 2017, http://www.sonyaparker.com/2014/05/once-you-learn-how-to-accept-truth-no.html

11. Parody of Jesus Loves the Little Children, sung by neighborhood kids, not found online
12. Sonia Ricotti, accessed June 19, 2017, http://www.values.com/inspirational-quotes/6986-accept-what-is-let-go-of-what-was-and-have
13. Squire Bill Widener quoted by Theodore Roosevelt, *Theodore Roosevelt: An Autobiography*, chapter IX, (The Macmillan Company, 1913)
14. Corrie ten Boom, *The Hiding Place*, (World Wide Books, 1971)
15. Robert Frost, Goodreads, accessed June 19, 2017, https://www.goodreads.com/author/quotes/7715.Robert_Frost
16. Muhammed Ali, BrainyQuote, accessed June 19, 2017, https://www.brainyquote.com/quotes/keywords/school.html
17. Sir Walter Scott, To Inspire, accessed June 19, 2017, http://www.toinspire.com/author.asp?author=Sir+Walter+Scott
18. Jean Piaget, quoted by Erika Krull, "Piaget – Play is the Work of Childhood," Family Mental Health, accessed June 19, 2017, https://blogs.psychcentral.com/family/2010/09/piaget-play-is-the-work-of-childhood/
19. Maurice Sendak, *Where the Wild Things Are*, (Harper and Row, 1963)
20. Thomas A. Edison, Brainy Quote, accessed June 19, 2017, https://www.brainyquote.com/quotes/quotes/t/thomasaed132683.html
21. Marlo Thomas, "A Christmas Story," Huffington Post, December 20, 2013, accessed June 19, 2017, http://www.huffingtonpost.com/marlo-thomas/a-christmas-story_2_b_4480924.html
22. Pope Francis, Solidarity With Sisters, December 14, 2012, accessed June 19, 2017, solidaritywithsisters.weebly.com/pope-francis-homilies.html

23. Benjamin Franklin, Values.com, accessed June 19, 2017, http://www.values.com/inspirational-quotes/6018-be-always-at-war-with-your-vices-at- peace-with
24. Sir Winston Churchill quoted by Leslie Potter, "Who Said That? Probably Not Winston Churchill." Horse Channel.com, January 28, 2013, accessed June 19, 2017, http://www.horsechannel.com/media/the-near-side-blog/2013/0128-winston-churchill-horse-quotes.aspx.pdf
25. Jean Anouilh, Notable Quotes, accessed June 19, 2017, www.notable-quotes.com/a/anouilh_jean.htm
26. Friedrich Nietzsche, Goodreads, accessed June 19, 2017, www.goodreads.com/quotes/30-that-which-does-not-kill-us-makes-us-stronger
27. Eleanor Roosevelt quoted by Henrik Edberg, "Eleanor Roosevelt's Top 7 Fundamentals for Making Life an Exciting and Wonderful Adventure," The Positivity Blog- Simple Tips and Habits That Work in Real Life, accessed June 20, 2017, http://www.positivityblog.com/eleanor-roosevelt/
28. L. Frank Baum, *The Wizard of Oz*, (Chicago, George M. Hill Company, 1900)
29. Mitch Albom, *The Five People You Meet in Heaven*, (New York, Hyperion Books, 2003)
30. Walter Anderson, Goodreads, accessed June 20, 2017, https://www.goodreads.com/author/quotes/278436.Walter_Anderson
31. Anne Frank, *Tales From The Secret Annex,* **originally:** *Verhalen rondom het Achterhuis* (Dutch) (The Netherlands, Contact Publishing, 1949)
32. Thomas Merton, *No Man Is An Island, (Shambhala Library, Penguin Random House, 2005)*
33. Clarissa Pinkola Estes, Habits For Wellbeing, "How Does One Know If She Has Forgiven," accessed June 20, 2017, http://www.habitsforwellbeing.com/how-does-one- know-if-she-has-forgiven/

34. John Muir, quoted by William Frederic Badè, *The Life and Letters of John Muir*, (Boston and New York, Houghton Mifflin Company, 1924)
35. Hans Christian Andersen, The Hans Christian Andersen Center, "What the Whole Family Said," accessed June 20, 2017, http://www.andersen.sdu.dk/vaerk/hersholt/WhatTheWholeFamilySaid_e.html
36. Plato, quoted by Philosiblog, "You can discover more about a person in an hour of play than in a year of conversation." March 6, 2011, accessed June 20, 2017, http://philosiblog.com/author/philosiblog/
37. Is. 61:3 *The Holy Bible, New International Version*, (Grand Rapids: Zondervan. House 1984)
38. Henry Wadsworth Longfellow, The Maine Historical Society, "The Rainy Day," Accessed June 20, 2017, http://www.hwlongfellow.org
39. Ralph Waldo Emerson, *The Conduct of Life*, (Boston, Ticknor and Fields, 1860)
40. George Bernard Shaw, IMDb, "Geroge Bernard Shaw Biography," accessed June 20, 2017, http://www.imdb.com/name/nm0789737/bio
41. Douglas Adams, *The Long Dark Teatime of the Soul*, (Portsmouth, NH, William Heinemann, 1988)
42. Patsi Krakoff, "The Magic Ratio of Positive and Negative Moments," accessed July 22, 2017, https://www.thedailycafe.com/

www.ingramcontent.com/pod-product-compliance
Lightning Source LLC
LaVergne TN
LVHW021816060526
838201LV00058B/3409